California
The Land Of The Sun

by

Mary Austin

California
The Land Of The Sun
by Mary Austin

ISBN: 978-93-60464-42-4

Published by

DOUBLE 9 BOOKS

2/13-B, Ansari Road
Daryaganj, New Delhi – 110002
info@double9books.com
www.double9books.com
Tel. 011-40042856

ABOUT THE AUTHOR

Mary Austin, a pioneering American nature author and social activist, made huge contributions to literature in the early 20th century. One of her incredible works is "California: The Land of the Sun." This book is a testomony to Austin's deep connection with the herbal global and her ardour for the landscapes of California. In "California: The Land of the Sun," Austin eloquently captures the essence of the Golden State, portray shiny graphics of its numerous ecosystems, from deserts to mountains. Her prose reflects a profound appreciation for the unique vegetation and fauna that outline California's geography, showcasing her keen observational capabilities and environmental consciousness. Beyond its naturalistic recognition, the book additionally delves into the cultural and social factors of California, providing readers with a holistic knowledge of the country's character. Austin's writing transcends mere description; it will become a party of California's splendor, each in its landscapes and its cultural richness. Mary Austin's legacy lies no longer simplest in her literary achievements but also in her advocacy for Native American rights and environmental conservation.

CONTENTS

I
THE SPARROW-HAWK'S OWN

For a graphic and memorable report of the contours of any country, see always the aboriginal account of its making. That will give you the lie of the land as no geographer could sketch it forth for you. California was made by Padahoon the Sparrow-Hawk and the Little Duck, who brooded on the face of the waters in the Beginning of Things.

There is no knowing where the tale comes from, for Winnenap the Medicine-Man who told it to me, was eclectic in his faiths as in his practice. Winnenap was a Shoshone, one of the group who had been forced southward into Death Valley when the great Pah Ute nation had split their tribes like a wedge. In the last of their wars he had been taken as a hostage by the Paiutes and brought up by them. He might have remembered the story, or his wife might have told him. She was a tall brown woman out of Tejon, and *her* mother was of that band of captives taken from San Gabriel by the Mojaves, Mission-bred. Wherever it came from, the tale has its roots deep in the land it explains.

Padahoon, being wearied of going to and fro under the heavens, said to the Little Duck that it was time there should be mountains; so the Little Duck dived and brought up the primordial mud of which even the geographers are agreed mountains are made.

As he brought it the Sparrow-Hawk built a round beautiful ring of mountains enclosing a quiet space of sea. Said the Little Duck, "I choose this side," coming up with his bill full of mud toward the west. Whereupon the Sparrow-Hawk built the other side higher. When it was all done and the Little Duck surveyed it, he observed, as people will to this day, the discrepancy between the low western hills and the high Sierras, and he thought the builder had not played him fair. "Very well, then," said the Sparrow-Hawk, "since you are resolved to be so greedy," and he bit out pieces of the Sierras with his bill, and threw them over his shoulder.

You can see the bites still deep and sharp about Mt. Whitney.

But the Little Duck would not be satisfied; he took hold by the great bulk of Shasta and began to pull, and Padahoon pulled on his side until the beautiful ring was pulled out in a long oval and began to break on the west where the bay of San Francisco comes in. So they were forced to divide the mountain range north and south and make what they could of it. But the Sparrow-Hawk, remembering the pieces he had thrown over his shoulder, chose the south, where you can still see him sailing any clear day about four in the afternoon, over all his stolen territory.

There you have the bones of the land as neatly laid out for you as they could do it in Kensington Museum: the long oval, breaking seaward, the high, bitten, westward peaks, and the Sparrow-Hawk's Own, tailing south like the quirk of an attenuated Q.

They serve, these fragmentary ranges, for the outposts of habitableness between the sea wind and the forces of pure desertness. Always there is skirmish and assault going on about them. Showers rush up the slope of San Jacinto, all their shining spears a-tilt. Great gusts of wind roar through the Pass of San Gorgiono, the old Puerto de San Carlos. Seasonally they are beleaguered by stealthy rushes of the fogs that from the Gulf hear the peaks about Whitney calling, or by the yellow murk of sand-storms on which the whole face of the desert is lifted up as it travels toward its destiny in orchard row and vineyard. Always the edge of the wind is against the stone. They shine, the frontlets of the sentinel saints, in that keen polish, as the faces of saints must with benignity.

Just beyond the pilæ of the broken mountains—the Pillars of Hercules of the West—the desert winds about the eastern bases of the range in deep indented bays, white-rimmed with the wave marks of its ancient sea. Out a very little way, where the shuddering heat-waves trick the imagination, it seems about to be retaken by the ghost of tumbling billows. Nothing else moves in it; nothing sounds. Plantations of growing things near the Pass lean all a little toward it, edging, peering—the wild, spiny, thorny things of the desert to enter the rain-fed paradise, the full-leafed offspring of the sea wind plotting to take the unfriended sandy spaces. They creep a little forward or back as the years run wet or dry. The green things stand up, they march along the cliffs, they balance on the edge of precipices, but desperation is in every contorted stem of *mesquite* and *palo verde*. And with all this struggle, so still! East on the desert rim the Colorado ramps like a stallion between its walls, westward the Pacific rings the low foreshore with thunder; but the land never cries out, quartz mountains disintegrate but they do not murmur.

It is odd here in a land rife with the naked struggle of great pagan forces, to find the promontories so lend themselves to the gentle names of saints. Perhaps the Padres were not so far from nature as one thinks; in the southerly range which, with San Bernardino on the north, sentinels the Pass by which the iron-rimmed Emigrant trail enters the coast valleys, they rendered for once the pagan touch. San Jacinto—St. Hyacinth—was he ever anything but a Christianised memory of a Grecian myth, or does it matter at all so long as there are men to see, in the deep purple light that dies along the heights, the colour of blood that is shed for love? Perhaps the best thing beauty can say to Greek or Christian is that there are still things worth dying for. No doubt the veins of Padre Jayme Bravo were as rich in martyr passion as the stained air of the mountain is in purples, paling to rose at morning, thinning at noon to pure aerial blues.

Seen from the coast the range has a finny contour as of some huge creature risen from the sea, with low hills about it like dolphins playing; but the prevailing note of the landscape is always blue, repeating the tints of the wild brodiæa that may be found on the lomas early in April, sending up its clustered heads between two slender curving spears.

Near at hand the masking growth is seen to be green, the dark olivaceous green of the chamisal. Nowhere does one get the force of the Spanish termination *al*—the place where—as in that word. The chamisal is the place of the chamise: miles and miles of it, with scarcely another shrub allowed, spread over the mesa and well up into laps and bays of the hills. It grows breast high, man high in the favoured regions; but even where under the influence of drouth and altitude it creeps to the knees, it abates nothing of its social character. Its ever-green foliage has a dull shining from the resinous coating which protects it from evaporation, and a slight sticky feel, characteristics that no doubt won it the name of "greasewood" from the emigrants who valued it chiefly because it could be burned green. The spring winds blowing up from the bay whip all its fretted surface to a froth of panicled white bloom, that, stirring a little as the wind shifts, full of bee-murmur, touches the imagination with the continual reminder of the sea. Higher up the thick lacy chaparral flecks and ripples, showing the light underside of leaves, and tosses up great fountain sprays of ceanothus, sea-blue and lilac-scented.

**SAN DIEGO, LOOKING ACROSS
THE BAY TOWARD POINT LOMA**

All the human interest of this region centres about the city on the bay of San Diego, a low locked harbour with a long spit of sand breaking the mild Pacific swell, as it bides its time for the shipping of the south-western world. It has already waited longer than most people suppose. Just fifty years after the landing of Columbus on the Bahamas, Cabrillo discovered it; Sir Francis Drake, romping up that coast with his buccaneers, must have seen it though he left no note of any visit, and in 1602 Sebastian Viscaino anchored there and gave it its present name. Just about the time the mixed Dutch and English on the Atlantic coast were beginning to think of themselves as Americans and to act accordingly, the Franciscan *Frailes* settled on San Diego bay. Nobody will know why it was reserved for the brown-skirted brothers of St. Francis to undertake the subjugation of Alta California, until it is known why the King of Spain quarrelled with the Jesuits. They were accused of plotting against His Majesty, but in those days it was possible to accuse the Jesuits of almost anything without going very far wrong in the popular estimate. I have my own opinion about it, which is that a great land, like a great lady, has her way with men. And no land has called its own as has California:—poet or painter or pioneer, the world's rim under. No better patron could be found for this blossoming West than Francis of Assisi, who preached to his little brothers of the air and would have made a convert of the coyote. Perhaps the first settlers of a country leave their stripe on all the land's later offspring: if it was a way the West took to breed fervour and faith and the spirit of prophecy in the young generation, who shall say she has not succeeded?

In January of 1769 two expeditions by land and sea set forth in the name of God and the King of Spain, under the patronage of Señor San Jose, indubitable patron of all journeys since the flight into Egypt. In April the ship *San Antonio* anchored in the placid bay, there to await the live stock driven up from Velicatá. So the old world came to the new with a whole collocation of sainted personages flocking like doves to her banners.

But it was not saints that the land wanted so much as the stuff that goes to make them. The expedition starved, sickened; their eyes were holden. Governor Portola, with the greater part of the expedition, made a long *pasear* on foot to find the lost port of Monterey, and came back, with armour rust on his doublet sleeves and nothing much gained beside, to declare the expedition a failure. But Padre Serra—Junipero Serra, father president of Missions, juniper of God's own planting, sapling of that stock of which the founder of the order had wished for a whole forest full—Padre Serra claimed a churchman's privilege. He demanded time for a *novena*, a nine days' cycle of prayer to the patron who was so unaccountably hiding the relief ship in the fogs and indecisions of the uncharted coast. It is my belief that the Padre chose the *novena* simply because it was the longest possible time he could hope to delay the return of the expedition. Nine days they drew in their belts and told their beads, and on the last hour of the last day, far on the sea rim, behold the white wings of succour!

The Patron, who could never be at a loss for an expedient, contrived that the ship should lose an anchor which compelled it to put in at San Diego, where they had no expectation of finding any of the party. It was so that the land tried them out and approved, for from that day the founding went forward steadily.

There is a fine growing city now on the site of the early landing, regularly stratified through all the architectural periods of California, from the low thick-walled adobe of the Spanish occupation to the newest shingle-stained bungalow of the latest one-lunged millionaire; but the land has not lost, in a century and a half, one mark by which the brown-skirted *Frailes* found their way about in it. It has its distinctive mark, the Sparrow-Hawk's land, the seal of a private and peculiar affection. Here about the mouth of one of its swift seasonal rivers, and touching as with a finger-tip the opposing shore of the island of Santa Rosa, is the habitat of the Torrey pine. Japanesque, unrelated, drinking the sea air, never spreading inland, it hugs the sea-worn edges of La Jolla, as though, as some botanists believe, the species came to life there out of the jewel-tinted water and the spirit of the desert dust.

It is also possible to think of it as a relict of the land of which the broken Channel Islands were made, but in any case it is a pity that science could not have retained for this lonely, restricted species the name the *Frailes* gave to its fostering waters, Soledad—the solitary. Behind the town the mesa rises abruptly, knife-cut by the gullies of intermittent streams; and far back where the mountains break down into foothills, and these into the lomas—little low mounds of detritus—the sea air collects all the blue rays of the diffused light and holds them there all day in the hollows, in memory of the sea from which they rose.

In April of the year of the Occupation the white panicles of the chamise would be tossing here and there, and the yellow violets run thin lines as of fire among the grasses. You would not believe there were so many yellow violets in the world as a day's riding will still show you. At this season, *islay*, the wild cherry, will be shaking out its fine white spray of bloom, the button willow begins, the sycamore, the buckthorn, *cascara sagrada*; the great berried manzanita, which shed its waxen bells as early as December, will be reddening its apples. Here also the chia, the true sage, the honey-maker, bread of the wild tribes, makes itself known by the penetrating pungent odour of its unfolding foliage. Binding all the leafy thickets, runs the succulent starry bloom of the megarrhiza that, from its hidden root, as large as a man's body, sends up smothering tendrils so sensitive to their opportunity that you have only to sit down beside them on one of these long growing afternoons, to find all their tips curling in your direction and the stems moving sensibly across the grass in the direction of support. As early as February the foot-long vines can be seen locating the nearest shrub or the cañon wall, farther away than you could detect it by any tactile sense. And how quickly, once the objective is sensed, the questing Force is withdrawn from the unsuccessful members! Perhaps this one to the right may keep on in the direction in which it has caught the invisible communicating thread from the nearest buckthorn, but the other three or four green tentacles, finding no invitation from any quarter, not only stop growing but seem to shrink and dwindle in the interests of the climbing brother. Sometimes in a particularly lusty growth, all the young vines will be drawn toward some conspicuous support, so that by the third day those that lay out starlike, with inquiring tips raised a little, delicately feeling, will swing through all their points to the one hopeful direction. These warm sensuous days toward the end of April, just after rain, when the very earth is full of a subtle intoxication, one has but to thrust a finger among the bourgeoning tips and tendrils of the megarrhiza to see them stir with live response. One must suppose, since the megarrhiza is of no discoverable use to anybody, that the Force uses it to its own ends, an ascending, uprearing Force, rehearsing itself for a more serviceable instrument.—This, however, is a digression; probably the Padres found no time for philosophising about anything, much less so useless a specimen as the wild cucumber.

What the Franciscans saw first in Alta California was what all pioneers look for in new lands—the witness of their faith. They saw the waxberry bush from which they were to gather the thin coating of the berries into candles for their improvised altars, saw the crepitant, aromatic *yerba buena,* and the shrubby, glutinous-leaved herb of the Saints, given to them for healing.

More than all else they must have seen in the month of the Virgin Mother, high on the altar slopes of San Jacinto and San Bernardino, the white thyrses of the yucca, called The Candles of Our Lord. Back where the green exclusiveness of the chamise gives place to the chaparral, the tall shafts arise. They grow in blossoming, the bells climbing with the aspiring stalk until as many as six thousand of them may hang pure and stiff along the lance-like stem between the bayonet-bristling leaves. Long after the white flame has burnt out, the stalks remain, rank on rank, as though battalions of Spanish spearmen had fallen there, holding each his spear aloft in his dead hand.

It is only back there where the yuccas begin, that the small, swift life of the mesa goes on, very much as it did in the days of the Spanish *Frailes.* The doves begin it, voicing the mesa dawn in notes of a cool blueness; then the sleek and stately quail, moving down in twittering droves to the infrequent water-holes. The rhythm of a flock in motion is like the ripple of muscles in the sides of a great snake. After them the road runner, *corredor del camino,* the cock of the chaparral, crest down, rudder aslant, swifter than a horse, incarnate spirit of the hopeful dust through which he flirts and flits. Then the blueness is folded up, it lies packed in the cañons, the mountains flatten; high in his airy haunts the Sparrow-Hawk sails, and the furry, frisk-tailed folk begin the day's affairs.

REDLANDS, LOOKING TOWARD SAN BERNARDINO RANGE

The secret of learning the mesa life is to sit still, to sit still and to keep on sitting still. The only other secret is to be learned in the wattled huts stuck like the heaps of the house-building rats in the dry washes, inwoven with the boughs of buckthorn and *islay*, except for size scarcely distinguishable from them. For the Indian has gone through all that green woof with the thread of kinship and found it an ordered world. He is choke-full as is the chamisal of wild life, of the tag ends of instincts and understandings left over from the days when he was brother to the beast—those sleek-bellied rats, stealing to lay another foot-long, dried stick to the characterless heap of their dwelling,—bad Indians to him, trying to remember their ways when they were men; that brown feathered bunch, in and out of the chia bush,— she was present at the making of man. Your aboriginal has the true sense of proportion: not size but vitality. You can cover the sage wren with the hollow of your hand, but you cannot hop so far for your size nor be so brave about it.

Very different from the spring flutter and fullness, must have been the look of the land in the year of the martyrdom of Padre Jayme Bravo, which was the year of Bunker Hill and the Republic. The green of the chamisal was overlaid then by the brown tones of its seeding. *Islay* had shed its crimson drupes; the cactus fires had died down to the dull purples of the fruiting prickly pear; the sycamores by the dwindling waters of the arroya had scarcely a palsied leaf to wag. The Mission had been moved, for what reasons must be guessed by whoever has had occasion to observe the effect of a standing army on the subjugated peoples, back from the sea marsh to a little valley of what is known now as Mission River. Sixty converts had come down out of the hills to receive the Medicine of the Soft-Hearted God. That is the way they must have looked at it—rood and cup and sprinkling water, and the bells louder than the medicine drums. Back in the dry gullies the drums would have been going night and day where the *tingaivashes*, the Medicine-Men, lashed themselves into a fury over this apostasy. Certain of the renegades heard them between their orisons; they fled back to the muttering roll and the pound of the dancing feet. In the night after that, eight hundred of the Dieguenos, clothed in frantic fervour and very little else, came down to make an end of the "long gowns." How the soul of Padre Jayme must have leaped up as he heard them yelling outside his unguarded hut: the appetite for martyrdom is deeper than all our dreaming. He ran toward them with arms extended. "Love God, my children!" he cried, and received their arrows. When it was reported to the Padre President at Monterey, "Thank God," he said; "now the soil is watered." It did indeed repay them such a crop of souls as any watering produces in that soil; but at

San Juan Capistrano, where a new foundation was in progress, they buried the bells and returned to the presidio.

Few people understand why Californians so love their Missions, the meagre ruins of them, scant as a last year's nest. But two priests, a corporal, and three men in the unmapped land with eight hundred angry savages—it is the mark of the Western breed to love odds such as that! It is not to the campanile at Pala nor the ruined arches of San Luis Rey that men made pilgrimages but to the spirit of enterprise that built the West.

All about the upper mesa there are traces, scarcely more evident to the eye than the Missions, that the inhabitants of it have been dreamers, dreaming greatly. I do not now refer to the court of San Luis Rey, from the roofs of which a joyous populace once cheered a governor of California in the part of toreador, in a neighbourhood where Raphael-eyed muchachitos who have never heard of the Five Little Pigs that Went to Market can still repeat you the rhyme that begins

> Up in Heaven there is a bull fight,
>
> The bull has horns of silver and a tail of gold.

Heaven enough under those conditions to the children of the Occupation! Nor am I thinking of a road on which, when there is a light wind moving from the sea, you can still hear at midnight the pounding feet of the Indian riders galloping down to the bay, only to see their beloved Padre blessing them from the ship's side in departing. I do not think even—because I make a practice of thinking as little as possible of a matter so discreditable to us as our Indian policy—of the procession of the evicted *Palatingwas*, even though the whole region of Warner's ranch is still full of the shame of it and the rending cry. The struggle of men with men is at best a sick and squalid affair for one of the parties; but men contriving against the gods for possession of the earth is your true epic. The brave little towns which start up there with their too early florescence of avenue and public square, the courageous acres which the vineyardist clears in the chamisal and the chamise takes again! All along the upper mesa, Pan and the homesteader keep up the ancient fight. And with what unequal weapons! The wild gourd, the bindweed, the megarrhiza, at the mere rumour of a cleared space, come beckoning and joining hands. Though he goes gunning all day without finding one young rabbit for his pot, the bark of the homesteader's orchard trees will be gnawed by them at the precise sappy moment. At dawn the quail may be heard with soft contented noises between the rows of bearing vines, plunging their beaks in the ripest berries. Then the mule-deer will spend the night in the carefully fenced enclosure, ruining the largest bunches with selective bites; after which the homesteader, if he is wise, will know that he is beaten. The mule-deer can go over any fence, though usually he prefers to go between the wires, which he can do without altering his stride. Detected, even at its most leafless, the antlered chaparral makes cover for him until, after hours of following, he is glimpsed at last, scaling at his stiff bounding gait some inaccessible rocky stair from which nothing comes back but the bullet's deflected whine. Now and then some pot-hunter who remembers when the mule-deer could be heard barking to the does in any deep gully, when the moon rose hot on the flushed trail of the October day, will tell you that there are no more of his kind on San Jacinto. But so long as there are homesteaders to be fended from the hill borders, the mule-deer will come back. And when the mule-deer is gone there will still be drouth. Let the coast currents swing out a few degrees, or the Gulf winds blow contrarily for consecutive seasons, and the stoutest homesteader fails. After a few years you can guess where he has been by finding the chamise growing taller in the ploughed places.

Incurable wild hills and wild sufficing sea, and the little strip between which they give to one another—Indian giving!—conceded by the years of rain and demanded back by drouth; shoals that the tide piles and the sea eats again! It lies like a many-coloured dancer's scarf, and hearts are still caught in its folds as in the days of the Spanish Occupation.

There's a stripe of aquamarine turning to chrysoprase, that's for the sea; amber then for the hollow cliffs of La Jolla and San Juan, smugglers' cliffs eaten well under the shore; a stripe of scarlet, spangled with viscid diamond dew, that's for the mesembryanthemums crowding the foreshore; pale green of the lupins with a white thread through it of the highway, green again for the chamisal, and blue of the mountains' unassailable sea thought.

Nature is a great symbolist; what she makes out of her own materials is but the shadow of what man in any country will make finally of his. San Diego by the sea dreams of a great sea empery. What by all the signs she is bound to produce, is a poet. There in the scarf-coloured, low shore is the vocal forecast of him in the night-singing mocking-bird. Especially in the fringing island of Coronado out of the waxberry bush he can be heard gurgling like a full fountain with jets and rushes of pure crystal sound. From moonrise on until dawn he scatters from a tireless throat, music like light and laughter. It is as impossible to close the eyes under it as in the glare of the sun. And if the moon, the measurer, be gone on a journey to the other side of the world, still he sings, all his notes muffled by the dark; he sways and sings, dozes and sings, dreaming and wakes to sing. So it should be with poets whether anybody wishes them to or not. "The lands of the sun expand the soul," says the proverb.

II
MOTHERING MOUNTAINS

It is all part of that subtle relation between the observer and the landscape of the west, which goes by the name of "atmosphere," that one returns again and again to the reality of Christian feeling in the Franciscan Pioneers, as witnessed by the names they left us—one of the most charming proofs, if proof were wanted, of the power of religion to illuminate the mind to a degree often denied to generations of art and culture. How many book-fed tourists rounding the blue ranks of San Jacinto to face the noble front of the Coast Range as it swings back from the San Gabriel valley, would have found for it a name at once so absolute, so understanding as Sierra Madre, Mother Mountain?

There you have it all in one comprehensive sweep: the brooding, snow-touched, virginal peaks, visited and encompassed by the sacred spirit of the sea, and below it the fertile valley, the little huddling, skirting hills fed from her breast. The very lights that die along the heights, the airs that play there, the swelling fecund slopes, have in them something so richly maternal; the virtue of the land is the virtue that we love most in the mothers of men. And if you want facts under the poetry, see how the Sierra receives the rain and sends it down laden with the rich substance of her granite bosses, making herself lean to fatten the valleys. The great gorges and swift angles of the hills which fade and show in the evening glow, are wrought there by the ceaseless contribution of the mountain to the tillable land. And what a land it has become! There have been notable kingdoms of the past of fewer and less productive acres. Yet even in the great avenues of palms that flick the light a thousand ways from their wind-stirred, serrate edges, is a reminder of the host of bristling, spiny growth the land once entertained. It is as if the sinister forces of the desert lurked somewhere not far under the surface, ready at any moment to retake all this wonder of fertility, should the beneficence of the Mother Mountain fail. The Padre pioneers must have felt these two contending forces many a time when they lay down at night under the majestic Sierra, for they named the first spot where they made an abiding place, in honour of the protecting influence, *Nuestro Señora, Reina de Los Angeles*, Our Lady the Queen of the Angels. There she hovered, snow-whitened amid tall candles of the stars, while south and west the coyote barked the menace of the unwatered lands. Now this is remarkable, and one of the things that go to show we are vastly more susceptible to influences of nature than some hard-headed members of society suppose, that in this group of low hills and shallow valleys between the Sierra Madre and the sea, the most conspicuous human achievement has been a new form of domestic architecture.

This is the thing that most strikes the attention of the traveller: not the orchards and the gardens, which are not appreciably different in kind from those of the Riviera and some favoured parts of Italy, but the homes, the number of them, their extraordinary adaptability to the purposes of gracious living. The Angelenos call them bungalows, in respect to the type from which the later form developed, but they deserve a name as distinctive as they have in character become. These little thin-walled dwellings, all of desert-tinted native woods and stones, are as indigenous to the soil as if they had grown up out of it, as charming in line and the perfection of utility as some of those wild growths which show a delicate airy florescence above ground, but under it have deep, man-shaped, resistant roots. With their low and flat-pitched roofs they present a certain likeness to the aboriginal dwellings which the Franciscans found scattered like wasps' nests among the chaparral along the river,—which is only another way of saying that the spirit of the land shapes the art that is produced there.

One must pause a little by the dry wash of this river, so long ago turned into an irrigating ditch that it is only in seasons of unusual flood it remembers its ancient banks, and finds them, in spite of all that real estate agencies have done to obliterate such natural boundaries. This river of Los Angeles betrays the streak of original desertness in the country by flowing bottom-side up, for which it receives the name of *arroya*, and even *arroya seca* as against the *rio* of the full-flowing Sacramento and San Juan. A *rio* is chiefly water, but an *arroya*, and especially that one which travels farthest from the Mothering Mountains toward the sea, is at most seasons of the year a small trickle of water among stones in a wide, deep wash, overgrown with button willow and sycamores that click their gossiping leaves in every breath of wind or in no wind at all. Tiny gold and silver backed ferns climb down the banks to drink, and as soon as the spring freshet has gone by, brodiæas and blazing stars come up between the boulders worn as smooth as if by hand.

Farther up, where the stream narrows, it is overgrown by willows, alders, and rock maples, and leaps white-footed into brown pools for trout. Deer drink at the shallows, and it is not so long ago that cinnamon bear and grizzlies tracked the wet clay of its borders. This is the guarantee that this woman-country is in no danger of too much mothering. No climate which is acceptable to trout and grizzlies is in the least likely to prove enervating; men and beasts, they run pretty much to the same vital, sporting qualities.

All that country which extends from the foot of the Sierra Madre to the sea, is so cunningly patterned off with ranks of low hills and lomas that its vastness is disguised, or rather revealed by subtle change and swift surprises as a discreet woman reveals her charms. This renders it one of the most delightful of motoring countries. The car swings over a perfect road into snug little orchard nooks as safe and secret seeming as a nest, climbs a round-breasted hill to greet the wide horizon of the sea, or a mesa stretching away into blue and amber desertness, which when adventured upon, discloses in unsuspected hollows white, peaceful towns girt by great acres of orange groves, or the orderly array of vines trimmed low and balancing like small, wide-skirted figures in a minuet. And then the ground opens suddenly to deep, dry gullies where little handfuls of the grey soil gather themselves up and scuttle mysteriously under the cactus bushes, and dried seeds of the megarrhiza rattle with a muffled sound as the pods blow about. Here one meets occasionally the last survivors of the old way of life before men found it: *neotoma*, the house-building rat, with his conical heap of rubbish; or a road runner, tilting his tail and practising his short, sharp runs in the powdery sand under the rabbit brush; here, too, the lurking desert shows its spiny tips like a creature half-buried in the sand, not dead, but drowsing.

A EUCALYPTUS GROVE

As artists know colour, and poets know it, this is the most colourful corner of the world. The blue and silver tones of the Sparrow-Hawk's land give place to airy violets, fawns, and rich ambers. It is curious, that obstinate preference which a locality has for colour schemes of its own adoption; man can break up and re-form them, but he can never quite overcome the original key. Here the bright, instant note of the geraniums that shore up the bungalows, even the insult of the magenta-coloured Bougainvillea is subdued by the aerial softness that lies along the hills like the bloom on fruit. The sheets of Eschscholtzia gold that once spread over miles of the San Gabriel valley, and still linger in torn fragments about Altadena, have been sheared by the plough, to vanish and reappear again in the solid globes of orange, distilled from the saps and juices of the soil.

One of the most interesting of the instruments by which the cultivated landscape has gathered up and fixed the evanescent greens that spread thinly yet over the uncropped hills in spring, is the eucalyptus. All the tints are there, from the olive greens of the chaparral to the sombre darkness of the evergreen oak; young shoots of it have the silvery finish of the artemisia which once gave the note of the mesas about Riverside and San Bernardino. No other imported tree has quite to such a degree the air of the *habitué*; one wonders indeed if it could have been half so much at home in Australia, from whence it has returned like some wandering heir to the ancestral acre.

It proves its blood royal by its facile adaptiveness to the prevailing lines of the landscape, taking the rounded, leaning outline of the live oaks on the wind-driven hills, or in sheltered ravines springing upward straight as the silver firs. Perhaps its most charming possibilities are revealed in the middle distance where, lifted high on columnar stems, its leaf crowns take on the blunt, flowing contours of the hills. At all times it has a beautiful resilience to the wind, bowing with a certain courtliness without compulsion, and recovering as if by conscious harmonious movement. The pepper tree, however, most magnificent specimens of which may be found lining the avenues of Pasadena, or in some unexpected corner of the hills marking the site of some old Spanish hacienda, is always an alien. It is like the Spaniards who brought it, perhaps, in its drooping grace, in the careless prodigality with which it sheds its fragile crimson fruits. Something of old-worldliness persists in its spicy odours, and in the stir of its lacy shadows; when the moon comes over the mountain wall and the wind is moving, there is the touch of mystery one associates with lovely señoritas leaning out of balconies. One fancies that the pepper tree will last so long as the dying race of Dons and Doñas, and with them will cease to be a feature of local interest.

There is hardly more than a trace in the modern city of Los Angeles of *Nuestra Señora, Reina de los Angeles*. The last time I passed through the old plaza, the streets of offence encroached upon it from the east, and a corner of the sacred precinct had been sacrificed to the trolley. The Church of Our Lady, over whose door may still be traced the fading inscription from which the city takes its name, was never a mission, but one of the six chapels or *asistencias* centred about the Mission San Gabriel. It was here the first expedition passed northward looking for the port of Monterey, on the day of the feast of Our Lady in the year when the Atlantic Colonies were making up their minds to fight the English. It was close to this spot and along Downey Street were enacted the most pitiful of all the tragic incidents which marked the recession of the aboriginal races. Bereft of their lands and the protection of their Church, they became a prey to the greed of the dominant peoples, and used regularly to be incited to drunkenness upon their wages on Sunday, arrested while in that condition, and sold each Monday morning for the amount of their fines to the neighbouring ranchers. Things like this lurking under the surface of commercial enterprise, as the desert lies in wait in sandy stretches, advise us that much of our insistence on democracy grows out of our inability to trust ourselves to deal equitably with our fellows under any other conditions. We can keep to the rules of the game we have set up more easily than to the unfenced humanities. Here in the old plaza full of sleepy light, which still retains the indefinable stamp of the people to whom to-morrow was always a better day for doing things, one sighs for the short-sighted self-interest which so wasted the native children of the soil.

But after all the land couldn't have loved them as it does the race for which it brings forth its miraculous harvests. Not that there weren't miracles in those days; in fact they began here, or rather at San Gabriel, six miles or so beyond the river which in those days was called Porcincula, a name that linked the old world with the new by way of the little chapel in Italy in which the beloved Francis received such heavenly favours. The miracle of San Gabriel relates to a display of a canvas presentiment of Our Lady, at the mere sight of which the wild tribes experienced exceeding grace. Looking up suddenly at the Mother Mountain brooding above the plain, it is easy to understand how the symbol of aloof but solicitous care came home to the primitive mind, always peculiarly open to suggestions of humaneness in nature.

The heads of the Sierra Madre are rounded, the contours of great dignity. The appeal it makes to the eye is of mass and line. Its charms, and it has many, of forested slope, leaping waters, and lilied meadows, do not offer themselves to the casual glance, but must be sought after with great pains. The bulk of the range is of warm, grey granite, clothed with atmospheric colour as with a garment. It borrows more from the sky than the sea, taking on at times an aerial transparency, the soul of the mountain about to pass trembling into light. Pinkish tones are discoverable in even the bluest shadows, and at times the peaks are touched with the rich, roseate orange of the Alpine-glow. But the variations of temperature and atmospheric conditions are not sufficiently pronounced to present themselves to the sense as the source of its aspects of tenderness, of majesty, of virginal aloofness. Rather such changes seem to be occasioned by palpitations of the Mountain Spirit, remote in sacred meditation, glowing, dimming, defining itself from within.

It may be that the immense vitality of the land, its abundance, the bursting orchards, the rich variety of native growth, somehow dwarfs the earliest impression of the Sierra Madre, since few, if any, gather at first an adequate idea of the actual mass and height it represents. It is only after appreciation of the really amazing activities of the Angelenos is a little dulled by familiarity, at early morning when the groves are sleeping and the bright plantations of the gardens lack the sun to flash their brilliance on the sight, or at evening when a sea mist covers the teeming land, one is prepared to hear that many of these peaks are higher than the Simplon, and that it would be possible to wander for months in the intricacies of its cañons without having time to grow familiar with a single one of them.

Sometimes the mere mechanics of the land, the pull of the wind up the narrow gorges as you pass, advises the open mind of power and immensity residing in the thinly forested bulks. Passing what appears a mere shadowy gulf in the mountain wall, you are aware of a murmurous sound as of the sea in a shell, and feel suddenly the push of the draught on your windshield like a great steady hand. In places above San Bernardino, the steady pouring of invisible wind rivers has swept the soil for miles and defied three generations of artificial plantations. And sometimes the mountain speaks directly to the soul. I recall such an occasion one late spring. We had been skirting the range toward Riverside all afternoon, having the fall of the land seaward always in view, noting how, in spite of the absurd predilection of men for square fields and gridiron arrangements, the main lines of cultivation were being pulled into beauty by the sheer necessity of humouring the harvest. It was that lagging hour between the noon splendour and the gathering of the light for its dramatic passage into night. The orange orchards lay dead green in the hollows, unplanted ridges showed scarcely a trace of atmospheric blueness; unlaced, unbuskined, the land rested. And all in the falling of a leaf, in the scuttle of a horned toad in the dust of the roadway, it lifted into eerie life. It bared its teeth; the veil of the mountain was rent. Nothing changed, nothing stirred or glimmered, but the land had spoken. As if it had taken a step forward, as if a hand were raised, the mountain stood over us. And then it sank again. While the chill was still on us, the grip of terror, there lay the easy land, the comfortable crops, the red geraniums about the bungalows. But never again for me would the Sierra Madre be a mere geographical item, a feature of the landscape; it was Power, immanent and inescapable. Shall not the mother of the land do what she will with it?

Entering the cañons of the San Gabriel, one is struck with the endearing quality of their charm. In a country which disdains every sort of prettiness, and dares even to use monotony as an element of beauty, as California does, it is surprising to find, cut in the solid granite wall, little dells all laced with fern and saxifrage, and wind swung, frail, flowery bells. Little streams come dashing down the runways with an elfin movement, with here and there a miniature fall "singing like a bird," as Muir described it, between moss-encrusted banks.

GLENDALE, VALLEY OF THE SAN GABRIEL

Into the open mouths of such cañons have retreated the hosts of wildflowers that once in the wet seasons overran all that country from San Bernardino to the sea,—the white sage, most honeyful of all the sages, the poppies, gilias, cream cups, nemophilias which twenty-five years ago were as common as meadow grass, as thick as the planted fields of alfalfa which have usurped them. Settlers who came into this country when the trail over the San Gorgiono had not yet hardened between iron rails, tell of riding belly deep for miles in wild oats and waving bloom, and where the trail goes out over the San Fernando, toward Camulas, the yellow mustard reached its scriptural height, and the birds of the air built their nests in it. Now and then in very wet years a faint yellow tinge, high up under the bases of the hills, is all that is left of the seed which, by report, the Padres sowed along the coastwise trails, to mark where they trod the circuit of the Missions.

Everywhere within the cañons, honeyful flowers abound, and up from the rocky floors the slopes are stiff with chaparral. This characteristic growth, which, seen from the open valley flooded by dry sun, appears as a mere scurf, a roughened lichen on the mountain wall, is in reality a riot of manzanita, mahogany, ceanothus, cherry and black sage, from ten to fifteen feet high, all but impassable. Elsewhere in the ranges to the north, the chaparral is loose enough to admit fern and herbaceous plants, carpeting the earth, but here the rigid, spiny stems contend for three or four feet, thick as the carving in old cathedral choirs, before they attain light and air enough to put forth leaf or twig. On the seaward side of the mountains, miles and miles of this dense growth flow over the ranges, parted here and there by knife-edge ridges, or by huge bosses of country rock, affording a great sweep to the eye, reaching far to seaward. From here the lower country shrinks to its proper proportion—a toy landscape planted with Noah's Ark trees—and the noise of men is overlaid by the great swells of the Pacific which come thundering in, lifting far and faint reverberations along the ranges.

On either side of these vast conning towers it is still possible to trace the indefinite tracks which wild creatures make, running clear and well defined for short distances and then melting unaccountably into the scrub again. Occasionally still they discover traces of the wild life in which the Sierra Madre once abounded. Deer are known to take advantage of such natural outlooks in protecting themselves from their natural enemies, and from the evidence of frequent visits here, bears and foxes and bobcats must have made much the same use of them. From such high escarpments the Indians would have seen Cabrillo's winged boats go by, and from them, all up the coast, ascended the pillars of smoke that attended the galleon of Francis Drake.

Once within the portals of the range, the granite walls sheer away from sequestered parks of oak, madroño, and Douglas spruce. The trees are not thickly set here as in the north, but admit of sunny space and murmurous bee pasture between their gracefully contrasting boles, and to a thousand bright-feathered and scaled things unknown to the all-pine or all-redwood forests. Such parks or basins vary from a few yards to an acre or two in extent, threaded like beads upon a single stream. One thinks indeed of the old-fashioned "charm string" in which each meadow space has its peculiar virtue:—open sunny shallows, arrowy cascades, troops of lilies standing high as a man's head, forested fern, columbine, delphinum, and scarlet mimulus along the water borders.

They grow slighter as the trail ascends—it is possible now to make nearly the whole distance in gravity cars for that purpose provided, but I recommend a sure-footed mule for the true mountain-lover—until above the source of the streams, from dips and saddles of the range, above the summer-shrunken glaciers, where the trees are bowed and the chaparral creeps as if awed and dizzy, it is possible to have a glimpse of the still unconquered and unconquerable "sage brush county." All along the back of the Sierra Madre wall the desert laps like a slow tide, rolling up and receding with the drouths and rains. The eye takes it in no less slowly than the imagination. It stretches, in fact, to the Colorado, but a haze of heat obscures its eastern border; long whitened lines of alkali, like wave marks, set the seasonal limit of its encroachments. Here and there shows the dark checkering of fertile patches, spilled over from the rich west-lying valleys; trending east by south lies the Sierra Madre like an arm, guarding the favoured region.

And yet in her very favour the Mother Mountain is impartial, for equally as she saves the south from desertness, she has denied to us the one instrument by which the desert could be mastered. Mighty as man is in transforming the face of the earth, he is nothing without the Rains.

III
THE COASTS OF ADVENTURE

Old trails, older than the memory of man, go out from the southern country by way of Cahuenga, by Eagle Rock, toward that part of the shelving coast where the Padre's mustard gold lingered longest, as if to mark the locality where the gold they missed was first uncovered. But suppose, on that day of the year '41, Francisco Lopez, *major-domo* of the Mission San Fernando, had not had an appetite for onions? Who knows how history would have made itself?

The speculation is idle; anybody named Lopez has always a taste for onions because they are the nearest thing to garlic. Señor Francisco,—I suppose one may grant him the title at this distance—rested under an oak and dug up the wild root with his knife, and the tide of the world's emigration set toward the Coasts of Adventure. I have, holding my papers as I write, an Indian basket reputed to be one of those in which, in those days, placer gold was washed out of the sandy loam; it was given me by one who had it from Don Antonio Coronel, and has a pattern about it of the low serried hills of the coast district. Where it breaks, as all patterns of Indian baskets do, to give egress to the spirit resident in things dedicated to human use, there are two figures of men with arms outstretched, but divided as the pioneers who carried the cross into that country were from those who followed the lure of gold. The basket wears with time, but the pattern holds, inwoven with its texture as Romance is woven with the history of all that region lying between San Francisco on the north and Cahuenga where, after a bloodless battle, was consummated the cession of California from Mexico.

A CAÑON IN THE SIERRA MADRES

From the white landmark of San Juan Capistrano to a point opposite Santa Inez, saints thick as sea-birds, standing seaward, break the long Pacific swell: San Clemente, Santa Catalina, Santa Rosa—their deep-scored cliffs searched by the light, revealing their kinship with the parallel mainland ranges. But there are hints here, in the plant and animal life and in the climate, milder even than that of the opposing channel ports, hints which not even the Driest-Dustiness dare despise, of those mellower times than ours from which all fables of Blessed Islands are sprung. Islands "very near the terrestrial paradise" the old Spanish romancer described them. Often as not the imagination sees more truly than the eye. I myself am ready to affirm that something of man's early Eden drifted thither on the Kuro-Siwa, that warm current deflected to our coast, which, for all we know of it, might well be one of the four great rivers that went about the Garden and watered it. Great golden sun-fish doze upon the island tides, flying-fish go by in purple and silver streaks, and under the flat bays, which take at times colour that rivals the lagoons of Venice, forests of kelp, a-crawl with rainbow-coloured life, sleep and sway upon tides unfelt of men. There are days at Catalina so steeped with harmonies of sea and sun that the singing of the birds excites the soothed sense no more than if the lucent air had that moment dripped in sound. These are the days when the accounts that Cabrillo left of his findings there, of a civil and religious development superior to the tribes of the mainland, beguile the imagination.

One thinks of the watery highway between the west coast and the channel islands as another *Camino Real* of the sea, where in place of mule trains and pacing Padres, went balsas, skin canoes, galleons, far-blown Chinese junks, Russian traders, slipping under the cliffs of San Juan for untaxed hides and tallow, Atlantic whalers, packets rounding the Horn, sunk past the load line with Argonauts of '49, opium smugglers dropping a contraband cask or an equally prohibited coolie under the very wing of San Clemente. So many things could have happened—Odysseys, Æneids—that it is with a sigh one resigns the peaks of the submerged range, paling and purpling on the west, to the student of sea-birds and sea-nourished plants.

Looking from the islands landward, the locked shores have still for long stretches the aspect of undiscovered country. Hills break abruptly in the surf or run into narrow moon-shaped belts of sand where a mountain arm curves out or the sea eats inward. And yet for nearly four centuries the secret of the land was blazoned to all the ships that passed, in the great fields of poppy gold that every wet season flamed fifty miles or more to seaward.

One must have seen the Eschscholtzia so, smouldering under the mists of spring, to understand the thrill that comes of finding them later scattered as they are, throughout the gardens of the world. I recall how at Rome, coming up suddenly out of the catacombs—we had gone down by another entrance and had been wandering for hours in the mortuary gloom—memory leaped up to find a great bed of golden poppies tended by brown, bearded Franciscans. They couldn't say—Fray Filippo, whom I questioned, had no notion—whence the sun-bright cups had come, except that they were common in the gardens of his order. It seemed a natural sort of thing for some Mission Padre, seeking a memento of himself to send back to his Brothers of St. Francis half a world away, to have chosen these shining offsprings of the sun. There was confirmation in the fact that Fray Filippo knew them not by the unspellable botanical name, but by the endearing Castilian "dormidera," sleepy-eyed, in reference to their habit of unfolding only to the light; but the connecting thread was lost. Channel fishermen still, in spite of the obliterating crops, can trace the blue lines of lupins between faint streaks of poppy fires, and catch above the reek of their boats, when the land wind begins, blown scents of *islay* and ceanothus.

No rivers of water of notable size pour down this west coast, but rivers of green flood the shallow cañons. Here and there from the crest of the range one catches an arrowy glimpse of a seasonal stream, but from the sea-view the furred chaparral is unbroken except for bare ridges, wind-swept even of the round-headed oaks. This coast country is a favourite browsing place for deer; they can be seen there still in early summer, feeding on the acorns of the scrub oaks, and especially on the tender twigs of wind-fallen trees, or herding at noon in the deep fern which closes like cleft waters over their heads. Until within a few years it was no unlikely thing to hear little black bears snorting and snuffing under the manzanita, of the berries of which they are inordinately fond. This lovely shrub with its twisty, satiny stems of wine-red, suffusing brown, its pale conventionalised leaves and flat little umbels of berries, suggests somehow the carving on old Gothic choirs, as though it borrowed its characteristic touch from an external shaping hand; as if with its predetermined habit of growth it had a secret affinity for man, and waited but to be transplanted into gardens. It needs, however, no garden facilities, but shapes itself to the most inhospitable conditions. About the time it begins to put forth its thousand waxy bells, in December or January, the toyon, the native holly, is at its handsomest. This is a late summer flowering shrub that in mid-winter loses a little of its glossy green, and above its yellowing foliage bears berries in great scarlet clusters. Between these two overlapping ends, the gaumet of the chaparral is run in blues of wild lilac, reds and purples of rhus and buckthorn and the wide, white umbels of the alder, which here becomes a tree fifty to sixty feet in height. It is the only one of the tall chaparral which has edible fruit, for though bears and Indians make a meal of manzanita, it does not commend itself to cultivated taste. More humble species, huckleberry, thimble, and blackberry, crowd the open spaces under the oak-madroño forests, or, as if they knew their particular usefulness to man, come hurrying to clearings of the axe, and may be seen holding hands as they climb to cover the track of careless fires. In June whole hill-slopes, under the pine and madroños, burn crimson with sweet, wild strawberries. The wild currant and the fuchsia-flowered gooseberry are not edible, but they are under no such obligation; they "make good" with long wands of jewel-red, drooping blossoms, and in the case of the currant, with delicate pink racemes, thrown out almost before the leaves while the earth still smells of winter dampness. Though nobody seems to know how it travelled so far, the "incense shrub" is a favourite of English gardens where, before the primroses begin, it serves the same purpose as in the west coast cañons, quickening the sense into anticipations of beauty on every side.

Inland the close, round-backed hills draw into ranks and ranges, making way for chains of fertile valleys which also fill out the Californian's calendar of saints. But, in fact, your true Californian prays to his land as much as ever the early Roman did, and pours on it libations of water and continuous incense of praise. Every one of these longish, north-trending basins is superlatively good for something,—olives or wheat, perhaps; Pajaro produces apples and Santa Clara has become the patroness of prunes.

Nothing could be more ethereally lovely than the spring aspect of the orchard country. It begins with the yellowing of the meadow lark's breast, and then of early mornings, with the appearance, as if flecks of the sky had fallen, of great flocks of bluebirds that blow about in the ploughed lands and are dissolved in rain. Then the poppies spring up like torchmen in the winter wheat, and along the tips of the apricots, petals begin to show, crumpled as the pink lips of children shut upon mischievous secrets; a day or two of this and then the blossoms swarm as bees, white fire breaks out among the prunes, it scatters along the foothills like the surf. Toward the end of the blooming season all the country roads are defined by thin lines of petal drift, and any wind that blows is alive with whiteness. After which, thick leafage covers the ripening fruit and the valley dozes through the summer heat with the farms outlined in firm green, like a patchwork quilt drawn up across the mountains' knees.

The tree that gives the memorable touch to the landscape of the coast valleys is the oak, both the roble and encinas varieties. There are others with greater claims to distinction, the sequoia, the "big tree," lurking in the Santa Cruz mountains, the madroño, red-breeched, green-coated, a very Robin Hood of trees, sequestered in cool cañons, and the redwood, the *palo colorado*, discovered by the first Governor, Don Gaspar de Portola, on his search for the lost port of Monte Rey. All these keep well back from the main lines of travel. The most that the rail tourist sees of them is a line of redwoods, perhaps, climbing up from the sea-fronting cañons to peer and whisper on the ridges above the fruiting orchards. But the oaks go on, keeping well in the laps of the hills, avoiding the wind rivers, marching steadily across the alluvial basins on into the hot interior. They are more susceptible to wind influence than almost any other, and mark the prevailing direction of the seasonal air currents with their three-hundred-year-old trunks as readily as reeds under a freshet. You can see them hugging the lee side of any cañon, leaning as far as they may out of the sea-born draughts, but standing apart, true aristocrats among trees, disdaining alike one another and the whole race of orchard inmates. When in full leaf, for the *roble* is deciduous, they are both of them distinctly paintable, particularly when in summer the trunks, grey and aslant, upbearing cloud-shaped masses of dark green, make an agreeable note against the fawn-coloured hills. The *roble* is a noble tree, high-crowned, with a great sweep of branches, but seen in winter stripped of its thick, small leafage, it loses interest. Its method of branching is fussy, too finely divided, and without grace.

THE CEMETERY, SANTA BARBARA MISSION

Around Santa Margarita and Paso Robles filmy moss spreads a veil over the *robles* as of Druid meditation; one fancies them aloof from the stir of present-day life as they were from the bears that used to feed on the mast under them. A hundred years or so ago the Franciscans drove out the bears by an incantation—I mean by the exorcism of the Church enforced with holy water and a procession with banners around the Mission precinct: "I adjure you, O Bears, by the true God, by the Holy God ... to leave the fields to our flocks, not to molest them nor come near them." But bears or *homo sapiens*, it is all one to the oaks of San Antonio; indeed, if legend is to be credited, the four-footed brothers would have been equally as acceptable to the patron of the Mission where this interesting ceremony took place. I can testify, however, that after all this lapse of time the exorcism is still in force, for though I have been up and down that country many times I have seen no bears in it.

Things more pestiferous than bears are driven out, humours of the blood, stiffness of the joints, by the medicinal waters that bubble and seep along certain ancient fissures of the country rock. This has always seemed to me the very insolence of superfluity. Who wishes, when all the air is censed with the fragrance of wild vines, to have his nose assaulted with fumes of sulphur, even though it is known to be good for a number of things? But there are some people who could never be got to observe the noble proportions of five-hundred-year-old oaks with the wild grapes going from tree to tree like a tent, except as a by-process incident to the drinking of nasty waters. So the land has its way even with our weaknesses.

SYCAMORES, A COAST RANGE CAÑON

Besides these excursions inland, which bring us in almost every case to one of the ancient Franciscan foundations, there are two or three ports of call on the sea front worth lingering at for more things than the pleasant air and the radiant wild bloom. One of these is Santa Barbara which Santa Inez holds in its lap, curving like a scimitar opposite the most northerly of the channel islands. Understand, however, that no good comes of thinking of Santa Barbara as a place on the map. It is a Sargossa of Romance, a haven of last things, the last Mission in the hands of the Franciscans, the last splendour of the Occupation, the last place where mantillas were worn and they danced the *fandango* and *la jota*; an eddy into which have drifted remnants of every delightful thing that has passed on the highways of land and sea, which here hail one another across the curving moon-white beach. Summer has settled there, California summer which never swelters, never scorches. Frost descends at times from Santa Inez to the roofs, but lays no finger on the fuchsias, poinsettias, and the heliotropes climbing to second-story windows. The wild thickets which connect the territory with the town, are vocal with night-singing mocking-birds; along the foreshore white pelicans divide the mountain-shadowed waters. The waters, taking all the sky's changes, race to the fairy islands, the chaparral runs back to the flanks of Santa Inez showing yellowly through the distant blue of pines; overhead a sky clouded with light. This is not a paradox but an attempt to express the misty luminosity of a heaven filled with refractions of the summer-tinted slope, the glaucous leafage of the chaparral, the white sand and sapphire-glinting water. The sky *beyond* the enclosing mountains has the cambric blueness of the superheated interior, but directly overhead it has depth and immensity of colour unequalled except along the Mediterranean.

Santa Barbara is a port of distinguished visitors; more, and more varieties, of sea-birds put in there on the long flight from the Arctic to the Isthmus than is easily believable. In the Estero—*esteril*, sterile—an ill-smelling tide pool lying behind the town, may be found at one season or another, all the western species that delight the ornithologist. The black brant, going by night, and wild swans, as many as a score of them together, have been noted in its backwaters, and scarcely any stroll along the receding surf but is enlivened by the resonant, sweet whistle of the plover. In hollows of the sands thousands of beach-haunting birds may be seen camping for the night, looking like some sea-coloured, strange vegetation, and early mornings when the channel racing by, leaves the bay placid, tens of thousands of shearwaters sleep in shouldering ranks that sway with the incoming swell as the kelp sways, without being scattered by it. One can see the same sight, augmented as to numbers, around Monterey, a long day's journey to the north as the car goes, long enough and lovely enough to deserve another chapter.

TALL CHAPARRAL, SANTA CRUZ

IV
THE PORT OF MONTEREY

Without doubt history is made quite as much by the mistakes of men as by their utmost certainties. The persistent belief of the ancient geographers in the existence of the Straits of Anian, the traditional North-West Passage, led to some romancing, and to the exploration of the California coast a century or so before it was of any particular use to anybody. It led also to the bluest bay. Viscaino took possession of it for Philip of Spain as early as 1602, nearly two hundred years before the Franciscans planted a cross there under Viscaino's very tree. During all that time the same oaks staggered up the slope away from the wind, and the scimitar curve of the beach kept back the brilliant waters. There is a figure of immensity in this more terrifying than the mere lapse of years. Not how many times but with what sureness for every day the sapphire deep shudders into chrysoprase along the white line of the breakers. We struggle so to achieve a little brief moment of beauty, but every hour at Monterey it is given away.

The bay lies squarely fronting the Pacific swell, about a hundred miles south of the Golden Gate, between the horns of two of the little tumbled coast ranges, cutting back to receive the waters of the Pajaro and the Salinas. From the south the hill juts out sharply, taking the town and the harbour between its knees, but the north shore is blunted by the mountains of Santa Cruz. The beach is narrow, and all along its inner curve blown up into dunes contested every season by the wind and by the quick, bright growth of sand verbena, lupins, and mesembryanthemums. The waters of the rivers are set back by the tides, they are choked with bars and sluiced out by winter floods. For miles back into the valleys of Pajaro and Salinas, blue and yellow lupins continue the colour of the sand and the pools of tide water. They climb up the landward slope of the high dunes and set the shore a little seaward against the diminished surf. Then the equinoctial tide rises against the land that the lupins have taken and smooths out their lovely gardens with a swift, white hand, to leave the beach smooth again for the building of pale, wind-pointed cones.

LOOKING DOWN ON MONTEREY AND THE BAY

The valley of the Salinas, which has its only natural outlet on the bay, is of the type of coast valleys, long, narrow and shallow, given over to farming and to memories of Our Lady of Solitude lying now as a heap of ruins in a barley field. It is a place set apart, where any morning you might wake to find the sea has entered between the little, brooding hills to rest.

Gulls follow the plough there, and pines avoid the river basin as though each of them knew very well their respective rights in it. One has, however, to make a point of such discoveries, for the entrance to the valley is obscured by its very candour, lying all open as it does to drifting dune and variable sea marshes.

It is even more worth while to follow the flat-bordered Pajaro into the shut valley where dozes the little town of San Juan Bautista, taking on its well-sunned mesa, those placid lapses of self-forgetfulness which are to the aged as a foretaste of the long sleep. Here it was that the magic muse of Music came into the country. It came in a little tin-piped, wooden hand-organ, built by one Benjamin Dobson of 22 Swan Street, London, in the year 1735, but of all its history until it was unpacked from mule-back by Padre Lausan in 1797, there is not a word current. Our acquaintance with it begins on the day that the Padre set it up in the hills and played, "The Siren's Waltz," "Lady Campbell's Reel," and all its repertoire of favourite London airs, of which the least appropriate to its present mission must have been the one called "Go to the Devil." Which only goes to prove that the spirit of the Franciscans was often superior to their means, for what the simple savages did do as soon as they had overcome their superstitious fear of the noise box, was to come to Mass to hear it as often as possible. There remain three old volumes of music written later for the Mission which came true to its founding and excelled in all sweet sounds, but none, it is said, pleased the Indians so much or so raised their spirits as "The Siren's Waltz." No doubt its inspiriting strains added something to the warlike spirit which led here to the only local resistance opposed to the American invasion, for it was on the Gavilan heights above the little town that Frémont, on the tallest tree that he could find, raised the Stars and Stripes, gallantly if somewhat prematurely. It was from San Juan that Castro's men marched to the final capitulation of Cahuenga, and finally from here the last remnant of the old life drains away. One hears the echo of it faint as the sea sounds that on rare days come trembling up the valley on the translucent air.

Returning to the bay, one finds all interest centering about the Point of Pines, a very ancient, rocky termination of the most westerly of the coast barriers. The Point, which is really a peninsula, is one of the most notable landmarks between Point Conception on the south and Fort Point at San Francisco. Its lighthouse stands well out on a rocky finger, ringed with incessant, clanging buoys; between it and Santa Cruz light is a roadstead for an empire. A windy bay at best, deep tides, and squally surfaces, the waters of Monterey have other values than the colourist finds in them. Sardines, salmon, cod, tuna, yellow tail run with its tides. At most seasons of the year whales may be seen spouting there, or are cast upon its shoals. At one time the port enjoyed a certain prosperity as a whaling station, of which small trace remains beside the bleaching vertebræ that border certain of the old gardens and the persistent whalebone souvenirs of the curio dealer. Lateen-rigged fisher fleets flock in and out of the harbour, butterfly winged; and all about the rock beaches creep the square-toed boats of the Japanese and Chinese abalone gatherers. Thousands of purple sea-urchins, squid, hundred-fingered star-fish, and all manner of slimy sea delicacies, these slant-eyed Orientals draw up out of the rainbow rock pools and the deeps below the receding surf. They go creeping and peering about the ebb, their guttural hunting cries borne inshore on the quiet air, seeming as much a native sea speech as the gabble of the gulls. So in their skin canoes and balsas the Indians must have crept about the inlets for as long as it requires to lay a yard or two of mould over the ancient middens of the tribe, as long as it takes to build a barrier of silver dunes half a mile seaward. Even at that distance the plough turns up the soil evenly sprinkled with crumbling shell which holds to the last a shred of its old iridescence. Far inland, past the Sierra Wall even to the country of Lost Borders, I have found amulets of this loveliest of the pearl shells, traded for and treasured by a people to whom the "Big Water" is a half-credited traveller's tale.

About five hundred yards outside the surf, from Laboratory Point, circling the peninsula to Mission Point on the south, the submerged rocky ridge has grown a great, tawny mane of kelp. Every year it is combed and cut by the equinoctial tides, and cast ashore in brown, sea-smelling wind-rows, and every year it grows again to be the feeding-ground of a million water-haunting birds. Here the Ancient Murrelet fattens for the long flight to the Alaskan breeding-grounds, and in the wildest gales the little nocturnal auklets may be heard calling to one another above the warring thunder of the surf, or when the nights are clear and the mists all banded low beneath the moon, they startle the beach wanderer with their high keen notes and beetle whirring wings. Long triangular flights of curlew drop down these beaches against the westering sun, with wings extended straight above their heads, furling like the little lateen sails come home from fishing. Sandpipers, sanderlings, all the ripple runners, the skimmers of the receding foam, all the scavengers of the tide, the gulls, glaucous-winged, ringbilled, and the species that take their name from the locality, may be found here following the plough as robins do in the spring. When the herring school in the bay nothing could exceed the multitude and clamour of the herring gulls. They stretch out in close order, wing beating against wing, actually over square miles of the ruffling water between Point Pinos and the anchorage. But any attempt to render an account of the wild, winged life that flashes about the bays of Carmel and Monterey would read like an ornithologist's record.

After storms that divide the waters outside the bay into great toppling mountains, in the quiet strip between the kelp and the beaches, thousands of shearwaters may be seen sleeping in long, swaying, feathered pontoons, shoulder to shoulder. The island rocks standing within the surf, from the Point of Pines all down the coast to Point Sur, are famous rookeries of cormorant. Watchful and black against the guano-whitened rocks, they guard their ancestral nests, redecorated each season with gay weed, pulled from the painted gardens of the deep; turning their long necks this way and that like revolving turret-tops, they beat off the gluttonous gulls with a devotion which would seem to demand some better excuse than the naked, greasy, wide-mouthed young. Warm mornings these can be seen stretching black-stemmed, gaping bills from the nesting hollows, waving this way and that like the tips of voracious sea anemones. Other rocks, white with salty rime, are given by mutual consent to rookeries of the yelping seals, the "sea lions" of this coast. Moonlight nights they can be seen playing there, with the weird half-human suggestion as of some mythical sea creatures.

Other and less fortunate adventurers on the waters of Monterey have left strange traces on that coast; one stumbles on a signboard set up among the rocks to mark where such and such a vessel went to pieces in a night of storm. Buried deep in the beach beyond the anchorage is the ancient teakwood hull of the *Natala*, the ship that carried Napoleon to Elba. It brought secularisation to the Missions also, after which unfriendly service the wind woke in the night and broke it against the shore. Just off Point Lobos, the Japanese divers after abalones report a strange, uncharted, sunken craft, a Chinese junk blown out of her course perhaps, or one of those unreported galleons that followed a phantom trail of gold all up the west coast of the New World. Strange mosses come ashore here, tide by tide, all lacy and scarf-coloured, and once we found on the tiny strand below Pescadero, a log of sandal-wood with faint waterworn traces of tool marks still upon it.

Most mysterious of all the hints held by the farthest west—for behold, when you have come to land again, sailing from this port, it is east!—of a time before our time, is the Monterey cypress.

Across the neck of the peninsula, a matter of six or eight miles, cuts in the little bay of Carmel, a blue jewel set in silver sand. Two points divide it from the racing Pacific, the southern limb of Punta Pinos, and the deeply divided rocky ledge of Lobos—Lobos, the wolf, with thin, raking, granite jaws. Now on these two points, and nowhere else in the world, are found natural plantations of the trees that might have grown in Dante's Purgatorio, or in the imagined forests where walked the rapt, tormented soul of Blake. Blake, indeed, might have had a hint of these from some transplanted seedling on an English terrace, for the Monterey cypress is quick-growing for the first century or so and one of the most widely diffused of trees; but only here on the Point and south to Pescadero ranch do they grow of God's planting. With writhen trunks and stiff contorted limbs they take the storm and flying scud as poppies take the sun. Incredibly old, even to the eye, they have no soil, nor seek none other than the thousand-year litter of their scaly needles, the husk of their nut-shaped, woody cones—the Spirit of the Ancient Rocks come to life in a tree. Grown under friendly conditions the young trees spire as do other conifers, but here they take on strange enchanted shapes. Their flat, wind-depressed tops are resilient as springs; one may lie full length along them, scarcely sunk in the minutely-feathered twigs, and watch the coasting steamers trail by on seas polished by the heat, or the winter surf bursting high in air. Or one could steal through their thick plantations unsuspected, from twisty trunk to trunk in the black shade, feeling the old earth-mood and man's primeval fear, the pricks and warnings of a world half made. The oldest of the cypresses are attacked by a red fungus rust, the colour of corroding time. It creeps along the under side of boughs and eats away the green, but even then the twisted heart wood will outlast most human things.

PESCADERO, A CHINESE FISHING VILLAGE, MONTEREY BAY

The pines of Monterey, though characteristic enough of the locality to take on its identifying name, are thoroughly plebeian: prolific, quick-growing, branching like candelabra when young; but in a hundred years or so their wide limbs, studded with persistent cones, take on something of the picturesque eccentricity that may be noticed among the old in rural neighbourhoods. They grow freely back into the hills till they are warned away from the cañons by the more sequestered *palo colorado*. The Monterey pine is one of the long-needled varieties, but of a too open growth perhaps, or too flexile to have any voice but a faint rustling echo of the ocean. The hill above Monterey, crowned with them, is impressive enough; they look lofty and aloof and dark against the sky, but growing in a wood they are seen to be too spindling and sparse-limbed to be interesting. The oaks do better by the landscape, all of the *encinas* variety, bearing stiff clouds of evergreen foliage in lines simple enough to compose beautifully with the slow scimitar sweep of the bay and the round cloud-masses that, gathering from the sea, hang faintly pearled above the horizon. There are no redwoods on the peninsula; straggling lines of them look down from Palo Corona on Carmel Bay, walking one after another, with their odd tent-shaped tops and long branches all on the windward side, like a procession of friars walking against the wind. On the Santa Cruz coast, and in small groups near Carmel, grows the tan bark oak, not a true oak, but of the genus *Pasania*, whose nearest surviving congeners are no nearer than Siam. How it came here, survivor of an earlier world, or drifting in on the changing Japanese current, no one knows. Apparently no one cares, for the only use the Santa Crucians have found for it is to tan shoe leather.

CYPRESS POINT, NEAR CARMEL

Three little towns have taken root on the Peninsula: two on the bay side, the old pueblo of Monterey with its white-washed adobes still contriving to give character to the one wide street; Pacific Grove, utterly modern, on the surf side of Punta de Pinos, a town which began, I believe, as a resort for the churchly minded—a very clean and well-kept and proper town, absolutely exempt, as the deeds are drawn to assure us, "from anything having a tendency to lower the moral atmosphere," a town where the lovely natural woods have given place to houses every fifty feet or so, all nicely soldered together with lines of bright scarlet and clashing magentas and rosy pinks of geraniums and pelargoniums in a kind of predetermined cheerfulness; in short, a town where nobody would think of living who wanted anything interesting to happen to him. Above it on the hill, the Presidio commands the naked slope, fronting toward Santa Cruz, raking the open roadstead with its guns. It was under this hill on the harbour side, where a little creek still runs a rill in the rainy season, that Viscaino heard the first mass in California, and nearly two hundred years later, Padre Serra set up the cross.

On June 30, 1770, that being the Holy Day of Pentecost, was founded here the Mission of San Carlos Borromeo, afterward transplanted for sufficient reasons, over the hill six miles away, on Carmel River. The town is full of reminders of the days of the Spanish Occupation, when it was the capital of Alta California. Old gardens here have still the high adobe walls, old houses the long galleries and little wrought-iron balconies; times yet the tide rises in the streets of the town, and still the speech is soft.

It is also possible to buy *tomales* there and *enchiladas* and *chile concarne* which will for the moment restore your faith in certain conceptions of a hereafter that of late have lost popularity.

Half a mile back from the beach, and divided from the town by the old cemetery, in a deep alluvial flat grown to great oaks and creeping sycamores, is situated one of the famous winter resorts of the world, Hôtel Del Monte. I can recommend it with great freedom to those curiously constituted people who have to have an excuse for being out of doors. The Del Monte drives and golf links are said by those who have used them, to provide such excuse in its most compelling form. Those who suffer under no such necessity will do well to take the white road climbing the hill out of old Monterey, and drop down the other side of it into Carmel.

From the top of this hill the lovely curve of the bay, disappearing far to the north under a violet mist, is pure Greek in its power to affect the imagination. Its blueness is the colour that lies upon the Gulf of Dreams; the ivory rim of the dunes, the shadowed blue of the terraces set on a sudden all the tides of recollection back on Salonica, Lepanto, the hill of Athens. You are reconciled for a moment to the chance of history which whelmed the colourful days of the Spanish Occupation. They could never have lived up to it.

But once on the Carmel side of the peninsula, regret comes back very poignantly. The bay is a miniature of the other, intensified, the connoisseur's collection,—blue like the eye of a peacock's feather, fewer dunes but whiter, a more delicate tracery on them of the beach verbena, hills of softer contours, tawny, rippled like the coat of a great cat sleeping in the sun. Carmel Valley breaks upon the bay by way of the river which chokes and bars, runs dry in summer or carries the yellow of its sands miles out in winter a winding track across the purple inlet. It is a little valley and devious, reaching far inland. Above its source the peaks of Santa Lucia stand up; for its southern bulwark, Palo Corona. Willows, sycamores, elder, wild honeysuckle, and great heaps of blackberry vines hedge the path of its waters.

SANTA CRUZ MOUNTAINS, THE COAST RANGE

Where the valley widens behind the low barrier that shuts out the sea, sits the Mission of San Carlos Borromeo, once the spiritual capital of Alta California. Here Junipero Serra, and after him the other Padre Presidentes, held the administration of Mission affairs, and from here he wandered forth on foot, up and down this whole coast from San Diego to Solano, with pacification and the seeds of civilisation. Here on the walls, faintly to be traced beneath the scorn of time, he blazoned with his own hands the Burning Heart, the symbol of his own inward flame. Here, in his seventy-first year, he died and was buried on the gospel side of the altar. It is reported that his last act was to walk to the doorway to look once, a long look, on the hills turning amber under the August sun, on the heaven-blue water and the white hands of the surf beating against the cliffs of Lobos; looked on the fields and the orchard planted by his own hand, on the wattled huts of the neophytes redeemed, as he believed them, to all eternity, after which he lay down and slept. It is further reported in the annals of the Mission that it was necessary to place a guard about the wasted body in its shabby brown gown, to defend it from the crowding mourners craving each a relic of the blessed remains. Had I lived at that time I should have been among them, for he was a great soul, and have I not felt even at this distance of the years the touch of his high fervours! San Carlos is one of the best-conditioned of these abandoned fortresses of the faith: the ancient pear trees are still in bearing, the wild mustard yellows in the fields, its architecture still betrays the uncertain hand of the savage; back in unsearchable recesses of the hills linger still some Indians whose garbled greeting is a memory of the *Ama Dios* which the padres taught them. Until a few years ago the prayer-post, a rude slab with the triple-knotted cord of the Franciscans carved around it, still stood on the hill at the end of the path their devout feet made, resorting to it for courage and consolation. These mementos fade, but year by year the impress of the great spirit of Serra grows plainer, like one of those trodden paths of long ago which show not at all if you seek them in the grass or near at hand, but from the vantage of Palo Corona are traceable far across the landscape.

The modern Carmel is a place of resort for painter and poet folk. Beauty is cheap there; it may be had in superlative quality for the mere labour of looking out of the window. It is the absolute setting for romance. No shipping ever puts in at the singing beaches. The freighting teams from the Sur with their bells a-jangle, go by on the country road, but great dreams have visited the inhabitants thereof. Spring visits it also with yellow violets all up the wooded hills, and great fountain sprays of sea-blue ceanothus. Summer reddens the berries of the manzanita and mellows the poppy-blazoned slopes to tawny saffron. Strong tides arrive unheralded from some far-off deep-sea disturbance and shake the beaches. Suddenly, on the quietest days, some flying squadron of the deep breaks high over Lobos and neighs in her narrow caverns. Blown foam, whipped all across the Pacific, is cast up like weed along the sand and skims the wave-marks with a winged motion. Whole flocks of these foam-birds may be seen scudding toward the rock-corners of Mission Point after the equinoctial winds. Other tides the sea slips far out on new-made level reaches, and leaves the wet sand shining after the sun goes down like the rosy inside pearl of the abalone.

The forests of Point Pinos are sanctuary. It is still possible to hear there at long intervals the demoniac howl of the little grey dog of the wilderness, "Brother Coyote," the butt, the cat's-paw, the Jack Dullard of Indian folklore, and sometimes in the open country below Point Lobos to see one curious and agaze from brown, naked bosses of the hills. Any warm afternoon, by lying very still a long time in the *encinal*, one may observe the country-coloured bobcat, tawny as the grass in summer, slipping from shade to shade. Sometimes if startled he will turn and face you with his blinking, yellow, half-hypnotic stare before he returns to his unguessed errand. Any morning you may find about your bungalow innumerable prints as of baby palms pressed downward in the dust, the tracks of the friendly little racoons who may be heard bubbling in the shallow cañons any moonlight night. Often I have left a cut melon under my window for the sake of seeing, an hour after moonrise, two or three of them scooping out the pink heart, spatting one another for helpings out of turn, keeping, in spite of the little gluttons you know them to be, a great affectation of daintiness. The night-cry of these little creatures is difficult to distinguish from the love-call of the horned owl, who on the undark nights of summer skims the low foreshore for the sake of the field-mice and gophers that feed on the seeds of the beach grasses. Every sort of migratory bird that passes up and down this coast lingers a while in the neighbourhood of Monterey, and some species, like the Point Pinos juncos, take from it their distinctive name. But if, when you walk in the woods, the Stellar jay has first sight of you, you will find them singularly empty, for these blue-jacketed policemen of the pines permit nothing to pass them unannounced. Of all the wood-folk, the wise quail alone ignores their strident warnings. The quail have learned not only the certainty of safety but its absolute limit. I have seen whole flocks of them, scared by the gun, whirring out of the public lands to a point not out of gunshot but within the forbidden ground, from which they send back soft twitterings of defiance. It is not, however, their habit to flush except in great danger, but to run to cover, moving with a peculiar elusive rhythm, like the rippling of a snake. This plump little partridge, for it is only in the common speech that he becomes a quail, is the apt spirit of the chaparral—cheerful, social, strong in the domestic virtues; his crest not floating backward in warrior fashion, but cocked forward over an eye, he has all the air of the militant bourgeois, who could fight of course, but finds that running matches better with his inclinations. Just at the end of rains, before mating begins, hundreds of them may be seen feeding in the flock on open hillsides, and the thickets of buckthorn and ceanothus ring with their soft Spanish *Cuidado!*—Have a care!

Three roads go up out of the peninsula to entice the imagination—that which we have already taken to the hills of Salinas and the little town of San Juan, the road to Carmel Valley, and the adventurous trail which leads all down the well-bitten coast past Sur and Pieoras Blancos. The Valley road turns off at the top of the divide between Carmel and Monterey; it passes on the landward side of the Mission into the river-bottom and skirts the narrow chain of farms, rising with the rise of the thinly-forested hills toward Tasajara, the Place of Springs. Here it is lost in the intricacies of the "back country." Deer-hunters go that way in the season, and those whose delight it is to lose themselves in the wilderness, to taste wild fruit and know no roof but the windy tent of stars. Years since there used to come out of that country shy-spoken, bearded men with bear-meat to sell and wild honey in the honeycomb, rifled from hiving rocks and hollow trees; but I fancy they are all dead now, or translated into the tall moss-bearded pines.

The coast road, after it leaves Point Lobos behind, goes south and south, between high trackless hills and the lineless Pacific floor. From the Point you can see it rise over bare, sea-breasting hills, and disappear in narrow cañons down which, it is reported, immeasurable redwoods follow the white-footed creeks almost to the surf. Dim, violet-tinted islands rise offshore to break the sea's assault. Now and then one ventures in that direction as far as Arbolado, to return prophesying. But the most of us are wiser, understanding that the best service the road can render us is to remain a dramatic and unlimned possibility.

V
OLD SPANISH GARDENS

Dona Ina Manuelita Echivarra had come to the time of life when waists were not to be mentioned. It took all the evidence of her name to convince you that her cheek had once known tints of the olive and apricot. Tio Juan, who sunned himself daily in her patio, had achieved the richness of weathered teak; his moustachios were whitened as with the rime that collects on old adobes sometimes near the sea-shore. But Dona Ina, who missed by a score of years his mark of the days of *mañana por la mañana*, was muddily dark, and her moustache—but one does not suggest such things of a lady, and that Dona Ina was a lady could be proved by a foot so delicately arched and pointed, an ankle so neat that there was not another like it in your acquaintance save the mate to it.

Once you had seen it peeping forth from under the black skirt—have not Castilian ladies worn black immemorially?—you did not require the assurance of Tio Juan that there was no one in her day could have danced *la jota* with Dona Ina Manuelita.

She would clack the castanets for you occasionally still, just to show how it was done, or with the guitar resting on the arm of her chair—laps were no more to be thought of than waists were—she would quaver a song, *La Golindrina* for choice, or *La Noche esta Serena*. But unquestionably Dona Ina's time had gone by for shining at anything but conversation. She could talk, and never so fruitfully as when the subject was her garden.

A Spanish garden is a very intimate affair. It is the innermost undergarment of the family life. Dona Ina's was walled away from the world by six feet of adobe, around the top of which still lingered the curved red tiles of Mission manufacture. It was not spoken of as the garden at all, it was the patio, an integral part of the dwelling. There was, in fact, a raw hide cot on the long gallery which gave access to it, and Dona Ina's drawn-work chemises bleaching in the sun. The patio is a gift to us from Andalusia; it is more Greek than Oriental, and the English porch has about as much relation to it as the buttons on the back of a man's coat to the sword-belt they were once supposed to accommodate. The patio is the original mud-walled enclosure of a people who preferred living in the open but were driven to protection; the rooms about three sides of it were an afterthought.

THE PATIO, OLD SPANISH RESIDENCE

The Echivarra patio did not lack the indispensable features of the early California establishment, the raised grill or cooking platform, and the ramada, the long vine-covered trellis where one took wine with one's friends, or the ladies of the family sat sewing at their interminable drawn work, *enramada*. The single vine which covered the twenty-foot trellis was of Mission stock, and had been planted by Dona Ina's father in the year the Pathfinder came over Tejon Pass into the great twin valleys. In Dona Ina's childhood a wine-press had stood in the corner of the patio where now there was a row of artichokes, which had been allowed to seed in order that their stiff silken tassels, dyed blue and crimson, might adorn the pair of china vases on either side the high altar. Dona Ina was nothing if not religious. In the corner of the patio farthest from the gallery, a fig-tree—this also is indispensable—hung over the tiled wall like a cloud. There was a weeping willow in the midst of the garden, and just outside, on either side the door, two great pepper trees of the very stock of the parent of all pepper trees in Alta California, which a sea captain from South America gave to the Padre at San Luis Rey. Along the east wall there were pomegranates.

A pomegranate is the one thing that makes me understand what a pretty woman is to some men—the kind of prettiness that was Dona Ina's in the days when she danced *la jota*. The flower of the pomegranate has the crumpled scarlet of lips that find their excuse in simply being scarlet and folded like the petals of a flower; and then the fruit, warm from the sunny wall, faintly odorous, dusky flushed! It is so tempting when broken open—that sort opens of its own accord if you leave it long enough on the bush—the rich heart colour, and the pleasant uncloying, sweet, sub-acid taste. One tastes and tastes—but when all is said and done there is nothing to a pomegranate except colour and flavour, and at least if it does not nourish neither does it give you indigestion. That is what suggests the comparison; there are so many people who would like to find a pretty woman in the same category. Always when we sat together nibbling the rosy seeds, I could believe, even without the evidence of the ankles, that Dona Ina had had her pomegranate days. Only, of course, she would not have smelled so of musk and—there is no denying it—of garlic. Thick-walled old adobes of the period of the Spanish Occupation give off a faint reek of this compelling condiment at every pore, and as for the musk, it was always about the gallery in saucers and broken flower-pots.

And yet Dona Ina was sensitive to odours: she told me that she had had the datura moved from the place where her mother had planted it, to the far end of the patio, where after nightfall its heavy, slightly fetid perfume, unnoticeable by day, scented all the air. She added that she felt convicted by this aversion of a want of sentiment toward a plant whose wide, papery-white bells went by the name of "Angels' trumpets."

On the day that she told me about the datura, which I had only recognised by its resemblance to its offensive wayside congener, the "jimson weed," the Señora Echivarra had been washing her hair with a tonic made of oil expressed from the seeds of the megharizza after a recipe which her mother had had from *her* mother, who had it from an Indian who used to peddle vegetables from the Mission, driving in every Saturday in an ancient caretta. I was interested to know if it were any more efficacious than the young shoots of the golden poppy fried in olive oil, which I had already tried. So we fell to talking of the virtues of plants and their application.

We began with the blessed "herb of the saints," dried bunches of which hung up under the rafters of the gallery as an unfailing resort in affections of the respiratory tract, and *yerba buena*, in which she was careful to distinguish between the creeping, aromatic *del campo* of the woodlands and the *yerba buena del poso*, "herb of the well," the common mint of damp places. When she added that the buckskin bag on the wall contained shavings of *cascara sagrada*, the sacred bark of the native buckthorn, indispensable to all nurseries, I knew that she had named two of the three most important contributions of the west to the modern pharmacopœia. This particular bag of bark had been sent from Sonoma County, for south of Monterey it grows too thin to be worth the gathering. The Grindelia, she told me, had come from the salt marshes about the mouth of the Pajaro, where Don Gaspar de Portola must have crossed going northward.

"And were you then at such pains to secure them?"

"In the old days, yes," she assured me. In her mother's time there was a regular traffic carried on by means of roving Indians in healing herbs and simples; things you could get now by no means whatever.

"As for instance — —?" I was curious.

Well, there was creosote gum, which came from the desert beyond the Sierra Wall, valuable for sores and for rheumatism. It took me a moment or two, however, to recognise in her appellation of it (*hideondo*, stinking) the shiny, shellac-covered *larrea* of the arid regions. There were roots also of the holly-leaved barberry, which came from wet mountains northward, and of the "skunk cabbage," which were to be found only in soggy mountain meadows, where any early spring, almost before the frost was out of the ground, bears could be seen rooting it from the sod, fairly burying themselves in the black, peaty loam.

But when it came to *yerba mansa*, Dona Ina averred, her mother would trust nobody for its gathering. She would take an Indian or two and as many of her ten children as could not be trusted to be left at home, and make long *pasears* into the coast ranges for this succulent cure-all. I knew it well for one of the loveliest of meadow-haunting plants; wherever springs babbled, wherever a mountain stream lost itself under the roble oaks, the *yerba mansa* lifted above its heart-shaped leaves of pale green, quaint, winged cones on pink, pellucid stems. But I had never heard one half of the curative wonders which Dona Ina related of it. Efficacious in rheumatism, invaluable in pulmonary complaints, its bruised leaves reduced swellings, the roots were tonic and alterative.

I spare you the whole list, for Dona Ina was directly of the line of that lovely Señorita who had disdainfully described the English as the race who "pay for everything," and to her mind it took a whole category of virtues to induce so much effort as a trip into the mountains which had not a *baile* or a *fiesta* at the end of it. Other things that were sought for by the housewives of the Spanish Occupation were *amole*, or soap-root, the bulbs of a delicate, orchid-like lily which comes up in the late summer among the stems of the chaparral, and the roots of the wild gourd, the *chili-cojote*, a powerful purgative. Green fruit of this most common pest, said Dona Ina, pounded to a pulp, did wonders in the way of removing stains from clothing.

Then there was artemisia, romero, azalea, the blue-eyed grass of our meadows, upon an infusion of which fever patients can subsist for days, and elder, potent against spells, and there was Virgin's bower, which brought us back to the patio, for a great heap of it lay on the roof of the gallery, contesting the space there with the yellow banksia roses. I had supposed, until the Señora Echivarra mentioned it, that its purpose was purely ornamental, but I was to learn that it had come into the garden as *yerba de chivato* about the time the barbed-wire fences of the gringo began to make a remedy for cuts indispensable to the ranchero who valued the appearance of his live stock. When the eye, travelling along its twisty stems and twining leaf-stalks, came to a clump of yarrow growing at the root of it I began at once to suspect the whole garden. Was not the virtue of yarrow known even to the Greeks?

There was thyme flowering in the damp corner beyond the dripping faucet, and pot-marigold, lavender, rosemary, and lemon verbena, all plants that grow deep into the use and remembrance of man.

No friend of our race, not even the dog, has been more faithful. The stock of these had come overseas from Spain—were not the Phœnicians credited with introducing the pomegranate into Hispaniola?—and thence by way of the Missions.

All the borders of Dona Ina's garden were edged with rosy thrift, a European variety; and out on the headlands, a mile away, a paler, native cousin of it bloomed gaily with beach asters and yellow sand verbenas, but there was no one who knew by what winds, what communicating rootlets, they had exchanged greetings.

Observation, travelling by way of the borders, came to the datura, which was to set the conversation off again, this time not of plants curative, but hurtful. We knew of the stupefying effects of the bruised pods and roots of this species, and—this was my contribution—how the Paiute Indians used to administer the commoner variety, called *main-oph-weep*, to their warriors to produce the proper battle frenzy, and especially to young women about to undergo the annual ordeal of the "Dance of Marriageable Maidens."

Every year, at the spring gathering of the tribes, the maidens piled their dowries in a heap, and for three days, fasting, danced about it. If they fell or fainted, it was a sure sign they were not yet equal to the duties of housekeeping and childbearing; but I had had Paiute women tell me that they would never have endured the trial without a mild decoction of *main-oph-weep*.

"It was different with us," insisted Dona Ina; "many a time we have danced the sun up over the mountain, and been ready to begin again the next evening...." But I wished to talk of the properties of plants, not of young ladies.

The mystery of poison plants oppressed me. One may understand how a scorpion stings in self-protection, but what profit has the "poison oak" of its virulence? It is not oak at all, but *Rhus trilobata*, and in the spring whole hillsides are enlivened by the shining bronze of its young foliage, or made crimson in September. But the pollen that floats from it in May in clouds, the sticky sap, or even the acrid smoke from the clearing where it is being exterminated, is an active poison to the human skin, though I had not heard that any animal suffered similarly. Dona Ina opined that there was never an evil plant let loose in the gardens of the Lord but the remedy was set to grow beside it. A wash of manzanita tea, Grindelia, or even buckthorn, she insisted, was excellent for poison oak. Best of all was a paste of pounded "soap root." She knew a plant, too, which was corrective of the form of madness induced by the "loco" weed, whose pale foliage and delicately tinted, bladdery pods may be found always about the borders of the chaparral. For the convulsions caused by wild parsnip there was the wonder-working *yerba del pasmo*. This she knew also as a specific for snake-bite and tetanus. So greatly was it valued by mothers of families in the time of the Spanish Occupation, that when a clearing was made for a house and patio, in any country where it grew, a plant or two was always left standing. But it was not until I had looked for it, where she said I would find it between the oleander and the lemon verbena, that I recognised the common "grease-wood," the chamise of the mesa country.

"But were there no plants, Dona Ina, which had another meaning, flowers of affection, corrective to the spirit?"

"Angelica," she considered doubtfully. Young maids, on occasions of indecision, would pin a sprig of it across their bosoms, she said, and after they had been to church would find their doubts resolved; and there was yarrow, which kept your lover true, particularly if you plucked it with the proper ceremony from a young man's grave.

Dona Ina remembered a fascinating volume of her mother's time, the *Album Mexicana*, in which the sentimental properties of all flowers were set forth. "There was the camelia, a beautiful woman without virtue, and the pomegranate——"

"But the flowers of New Spain, Dona Ina, was there nothing of these?" I insisted.

"Of a truth, yes, there was the cactus flower, not the opunta, the broad-leaved spiny sort, of which hedges were built in the old days, but the low, flamy-blossomed, prickly variety of hot sandy places. If a young man wore such a one pinned upon his velvet jacket it signified, 'I burn for you.'"

"And if he wore no flower at all, how then?"

Dona Ina laughed, "*Si me quieros, no me quieros*"; she referred to the common yellow composite which goes by the name of "sunshine," or in the San Joaquin, where miles of it mixed with blue phacelias brighten with the spring, as "fly-flower." "In the old Spanish playing-cards," said Dona Ina, "the Jack of spades had such a one in his hand, but when I was a girl no caballero would have been caught saying, 'Love me, love me not!' They left all that to the señoritas."

There was a Castilian rose growing beside me. Now a Castilian rose is not in the least what you expect it to be. It is a thick, cabbagy florescence, the petals short and not recurved, the pink hardly deeper than that of the common wild rose, the leafage uninteresting. One has to remember that it distinguished itself long before the time of the tea and garden hybrids, and, I suspect, borrowed half its charm from the faces it set off. For there was never but one way in the world for a rose to be worn, and that is the way Castilian beauties discovered so long ago that centuries have not made any improvement in it. Set just behind the ear and discreetly veiled by the mantilla, it suggests the effulgent charm of Spain, tempered by mystery. The Señora Echivarra had followed my glance, and nodded acquiescence to my thought. "In dressing for a *baile,* one would have as soon left off the rose as one's fan. One wore it even when the dress was wreathed with other flowers."

"And did you, then, go wreathed in flowers?"

"Assuredly; from the garden if we had them, or from the field. I remember once I was all blue larkspurs, here and here ..." she illustrated on her person, "and long flat festoons of the *yerba buena* holding them together."

"It would have taken hoop skirts for that?" I opined.

"That also. It was the time that the waltz had been learned from the officers of the American ships, and we were quite wild about it. The good Padre had threatened to excommunicate us all if we danced it ... but we danced ... we danced...." Dona Ina's pretty feet twitched reminiscently. The conversation wandered a long time in the past before it came back to the patio lying so still, divided from the street by the high wall, the clouding fig, and the gnarly pear tree. Beyond the artichokes a low partition wall shut off the vegetable plot; strings of chili reddened against it. There was not a blade of grass in sight, only the flat, black adobe paths worn smooth by generations of treading, house and enclosing walls all of one earth.

"But if so much came into the garden from the field, Señora, did nothing ever go out?"

Ah, yes, yes—the land is gracious; there was mustard of course, and pepper grass and horehound, blessed herb, which spread all over the west with healing. The pimpernel, too, crept out of the enclosing wall, and the tree mallow which came from the Channel Islands by way of the gardens and has become a common hedge plant on the sandy lands about the bay of San Francisco. Along streams which ran down from the unfenced gardens of the *Americanos*, callas had domesticated themselves and lifted their pure white spathes serenely amid a tangle of mint and wild blackberries and painted cup. The almond, the rude stock on which the tender sorts were grafted, if allowed to bear its worthless bitter nuts would take to hillsides naturally. It is not, after all, walls which hold gardens but water. This is all that constrains the commingling of wild and cultivated species; they care little for man, their benefactor. Give them water, said Dona Ina, and they come to your door like a fed dog, or if you like the figure better, like grateful children. They repay you with sweetness and healing.

A swift darted among the fig, marigolds, and portulacca of the inevitable rock-work which was the pride of the old Spanish gardens. Great rockets of tritoma flamed against the wall, on the other side of which traffic went unnoted and unsuspecting.

"But we, Dona Ina, we Americans, when we make a garden, make it in the sight of all so that all may have pleasure in it."

"Eh, the *Americanos* ..." she shrugged; she moved to give a drink to the spotted musk, flowering in a chipped saucer; the subject did not interest her; her thought, like her flowers, had grown up in an enclosure.

THE GOLDEN GATE AND BLACK POINT, FROM HYDE STREET, SAN FRANCISCO. (SITE OF THE PANAMA EXPOSITION, 1915)

VI
THE LAND OF THE LITTLE DUCK

Where the twin rivers set back the tides from the bay, the Land of the Little Duck begins. The tides come head-on past the Golden Gate and the river answers to their tremendous compulsion far inland, past the point where the Sacramento and San Joaquin flow together. On the lee side of the headland which makes the southern pilaster of the Gate, sits San Francisco, making of the name she borrowed from the bay a new and distinguished thing, as some women do with their husbands' titles. A better location for a city is Carquinez Strait; the Mexican comandante resident at Sonoma would have had it there, bearing the name of his wife, Francesca. Said he to the newly arrived American authorities, "Do so, and I will furnish you the finest site in the world, with State house and Residence complete." But it appears the land has chosen its own name.

All the years after the Pope had divided the New World between Spain and the Portuguese, the harbour lay hidden. Cabrillo, Drake, Maldonado, Juan de Fuca, Viscaino passed it in the night or veiled in obscuring fogs. And then Saint Francis showed it clear and lovely to Don Gaspar Portola, having for that revelation led him with holden eyes past his journey's objective. Likewise, when the time was ripe, he put it into the mind of the Yankee alcalde at Yerba Buena, a trading-post in the neighbourhood of Mission Dolores, that if the hamlet should be called San Francisco it might catch by implication the vessels clearing all ports of the world for San Francisco bay.

O Chance, Chance! says the historian and turns another page. But it is my opinion that among the birds to which Saint Francis preached was included the Little Duck.

The piers of the city front east, they face the Berkeley Hills, the Oaklands, the lands of the Sycamore, or, as the first settlers named them, the Alamedas. From thence vast settlements take their name, feeding the city as sea-birds do, from their own breasts. Back and forth between them the shuttling ferries weave thin webs of glistening wakes, duck-bodied tugs chugg and scuttle, busy still at world-building. From the promontory which makes the northern barrier of the Gate, Tamalpias swims out of atmospheric blueness. On its seaward slope, hardly out of reach of the siren's bellowing note, Muir Park preserves the ancient forest, rooted in the litter of a thousand years. And round about the foot of city and mountain the waters of the bay are blue, the hills are bluer. The hills melt down to greenness in the spring, the water runs to liquid emerald, flashing amber; the hills are tawny after rains, the waters tone to the turbid, clayey river-floods; land and sea they pursue one another as lovers through changing moods of colour; they have mists for mystery between revealing suns. Unless these things count for something, San Francisco is the very worst site in the world for a city. You take your heart in your mouth every time you go out to afternoon tea in the tram-cars that dip and swing like cockles at sea. They cut across streets so steep that grass grows between the cobbles where no traffic ever passes, to plunge down lanes of dwellings perched precariously as sea-birds' nests on the bare bones of hills that for true hilliness shame Rome's imperial seven. The bay side of the peninsula is mud, the Pacific side is sand. There great wasteful dunes blow up, they shift and pile, they take the contours of the wind-lashed waters—the very worst site in the world for a great city's pleasure-ground, and yet somehow it is there.

For this city is one of those which have souls; it is a spirit sitting on a height, taking to itself form and the offices of civilisation. This is a thing that we know, because we have seen the land shake it as a terrier shakes a rat, until the form of the city was broken; it dissolved in smoke and flame. And then as a polyp of the sea draws out of the fluent water form and perpetuity for itself, we saw our city draw back its shapes of wood and stone, and statelier, more befitting a spirit that has endured so much. Nobody knows really what a city is except that it is something more than a collocation of houses. From Telegraph Hill, where the old semaphore stood, which signalled the far-between arrivals of ships around the Horn, you can see the trade of the world pass and repass the pillars of the Gate, the wall-sided warships. But none of these things really explain how San Francisco came to be clinging there to the leeward of a windy spit of land, like a great, grey sea-bird with palpitating wings.

TAMALPIAS

True to her situation, San Francisco is nothing if not dramatic. One recalls that the earliest foundation was dedicated to Our Lady of Dolors, *Nuestro Señora de Dolores*; the Indians fought here as they did nowhere else against Christian dominion. There were more burials than baptisms, and in the old cemetery of Yerba Buena the dead were so abandoned of all grace that the sand refused to hold them. One who spent his boyhood in the shifting purlieus of the old Laguna told me how in the hollows where the scrub oaks shrugged off the wind and the sand waved like water, the nameless coffins were covered and uncovered between a night and day. But if the dead could not hold their tenancy, the living succeeded. They did it by the very force of that dramatic instinct awakened by the plot and counterplot of natural forces.

No Greek tragedy moved to more relentless measures than the moral upheaval of '56, when the whole city, in solemn funeral train behind the victim of one of those wild outbursts of lawlessness peculiar to the "gold rush," saw the lifeless bodies of the perpetrators hanging from the upper windows of the Vigilance Committee. Fifty years later came a wilder rout, down streets searched out by fire, snatching at humour as they ran, as so many points of contact for the city's rebuilding.

The very worst location in the world, as I have remarked, is this windy promontory past which the grey tides race, but so long as a city can dramatise itself, one situation will do as well as another in which to render itself immortal.

The bay of San Francisco with its contingencies is one of the most interesting of inland yachting waters, full of adventurous weather. It is possible to sail in one general direction from Alviso to the city of Sacramento, a hundred and fifty miles, and that without attempting the thousand miles of estuary and slough through which the waters slink and wind.

At this season of the year the river is pushed backward by the tide a matter of ten miles or more above Sacramento City: on the San Joaquin it is felt as far as Crow's Landing. At Antioch it begins to be saltish, and down through Suisun and Carquinez the river-water fights its way as far as San Pablo before its identity is wholly lost. At flood-times it may be traced, a yellowish, turgid streak, as far as Alcatraz. This is the islet of the albatross which lies south of the tide race, as Tiburon is on the north, fragments all of them of that salt-rimed ledge outside the gate where hoarse sea-lions play, and brother to the castellated cloud far along on the sea's horizon, the very capital of the kingdom of the Little Duck.

MILL VALLEY, AND BACKWATER OF SAN FRANCISCO BAY

The Faralone Light is the last dropped astern by the Island steamships sagging south to the equator; it is also the sea-birds' city of refuge. This is the great murre rookery of the west coast, and formerly thousands of dozens of eggs were regularly taken from the Faralones to the San Francisco market; but since the islands became a Government station the murres have no enemy but the pirates of the air. In clefts and ledges close against the wall-sided cliffs they defend their shallow nests against the sheering gulls, or, hard beset, will push their single, new-hatched nestling into the friendlier sea, darting to break its fall with incredible swiftness, for a swimming gait is one of the things that come out of the shell with the native-born at the Faralones. On the same shelving rocks puffins rear their ratty young in burrows or under sheltering boulders, and the ashy petrel, the "little Peter" of the sea, walking by night before the storm, comes ashore here to hide his seldom nest. On the south Faralone the fierce cormorant builds her house of painted weed, which often the gulls steal from her as fast as she brings it ashore, for the gulls are the grafters of the sea-birds' city. This particular variety, known as the western gull, neither fishes for himself nor forages for building material. He feeds on the eggs and nestlings of his neighbours, or waits to snatch the day's catch from the beak that brought it up from the sea. He has the virtue of all predatory classes, an exemplary domesticity. His nest is soft and clean, his nestlings handsome. The western gull is often found marauding far up the estuary of Sacramento, but it is his congener, the herring gull, who follows the long white wake the ferries make ploughing the windy bay; or, distinguished among the silent shore birds for multitude and clamour, scavenges its reedy borders.

Except for the promontories north and south, and the bold front of the Berkeley Hills opposing the Gate, the inland borders of the bay are flat tide-lands and sea-smelling lagunas. Stilts, avocets, herons, all the waders that haunt this coast or visit it in their seasonal flights, may be seen stalking the shallows for minnows, or where the marsh grass reddens, poised like some strange tide-land blossom, lifted on two slender stems. Low over them any clear day may be seen the grey old marsh hawk sailing, or the "duck hawk," the peregrine of falconry, following fiercely in the wake of the migrating hordes of water-fowl. All about Alviso the guttural cry of the black-crowned night-heron sounds eerily above the marshes, along with the peculiar "pumping" love-song of the bittern.

For some reason the air of the marshes is friendly to the mistletoe infesting the oaks and sycamores which stand back from the tide-line; but the marshes themselves are treeless. They have their own sorts of growth, cane and cat-tails and tule, goosefoot, samphire, and the tasselled sedges. This samphire of Shakespeare, *l'herbe de Saint Pierre* of the Normandy Marshes, is the glory of the Franciscan tide-lands; miles of it, barely above the level of the slow-moving water, spread a magic carpet of blending crimsons, purples, and bronzes. Under the creeping mists and subject to the changes of the water, beaten to gold and copper under the sun, it redeems the flat lines of the landscape with a touch of Oriental splendour.

For it is a flat kingdom, that of the Little Duck—the hills hanging remotely on the horizon, the few trees and scattered hugging the low shore of the sloughs as the shipwrecked cling to their rafts, desperate of rescue.

The rich web of the samphire, the shifting colour of the water, faintly reminiscent of Venice, borrow another foreign touch from the names under which the borders recommended themselves to attention: — Sausalito, "little willows," Tiburon, Corta Madero, San Quentin, San Raphael. Approached from the water, these names, with the exception of San Quentin, do no more than stir the imagination. San Quentin, on one of those courtesy islands newly rescued from the primordial mud, shows itself uncompromisingly for what it is, one of those places for the sequestration of public offenders, which is itself such an offence to our common humanity — to say nothing of our common sense. Free tides, free sails go by, and long, untrammelled lines of birds; south above the blue bay and bluer shore, the ethereal blue dome of Diablo lifts into the free air. Across the upper end of San Pablo Bay, which is really the north arm of the bay of San Francisco extending inland, Mare Island lies so low on the water that if it had not been made a naval reserve station it is difficult to know to what other use it could be put. One expects to have the land dip and swing from under like the ship's deck. It is in line with the guns which lie beside the Gate like watchful, muzzle-pointed dogs, and commands the whole upper bay and the opposing bluffs of Contra Costa in a manner highly commendable to those curious persons whose chief excitement lies in anticipating an Asiatic invasion. Nevertheless, along with the bastions of San Quentin it strikes, somehow, the note of human distrust amid all this charm of light and line and elusive colour, as if suddenly one should discover the tip of a barbed tail under the skirt of some seductive stranger.

Between San Quentin and the Straits, all about the curve of the bay, winding, wide-mouthed sloughs give access to a land as fertile as Egypt. A slough is a mere wallow of unprofitable waters, waters unused by men and still reluctant of the sea. Pushed aside by the compelling tides, too undisciplined to make proper banks for themselves, they are neglected by all but a few fringing willows and shapeless sycamores in which the herons nest.

Often at evening the white-faced ibis can be seen flying in long, voiceless lines, just clearing the twilight-tinted water, to their accustomed night perches in the wind-beaten willows. They return there, if undisturbed, year after year, accompanied in few and far-between seasons by the egret and the snowy heron, grown man-shy, or if they but knew the purpose for which their nuptial plumage is sacrificed, woman-shy, and seldom seen even by the most wishful eyes.

At Napa a few bull-headed oaks come down almost to the tide-line, and in Sonoma a clump of alien blue gums huddles aloof and unregarded, but from the water little is visible beside the stilted cabins of some gun club or the ramshackle resorts of the flat-nosed, slow craft that wind on mysterious errands between the sunken lands. Whole families of half-amphibious humans appear to live comfortably on these drifting scows, but one never by any chance catches them doing any distinctive thing.

The waters of the sloughs come down from the little inland valleys, where summer nests and broods in a blue haze along the redwood-serried hills. Whether it is white with cherry bloom at Napa, or purple with winy clusters at Sonoma, there is always something interesting going on there of the large process by which granite mountains are made food for man. It is worth a visit if only to learn that a country which does that sort of thing supremely well, finds it also worth while to do it beautifully. Yachting off San Rafael, it is possible to catch at times the scent of roses on an off-shore wind above the salt smell of the marshes.

The last rip of the tide is through the Straits of Carquinez into the back-water of Suisun. From here on, it is a rhythmic heaving to and fro as of well-matched wrestlers, the river-water is set back to Crow's Landing on the San Joaquin, and miles above Sacramento it returns again past Antioch and the Suisun islands. It is lost in a wilderness of tules, through which the sluggish currents blindly wind. Here we have nothing to do with men, our business is all with the tribe of the Little Duck: mallard, teal, tern, coot, heron, eared grebe, and awkward loon.

The tule is a round leafless reed. It springs up along the tide-lands or in the stagnant back-water of the rivers, or by any least dribble of a desert spring. No condition daunts it but absolute dearth of water; far-called, it travels on the wind over mountain ranges, over great wastes of waterless plain to find the one absolute condition, a pool — white rimmed with alkali or poisonous green with arsenic. I have seen it flourish by springs so charged with mineral that each slender column is ringed with its stony deposit, but I do not recall any standing water where tules are not. The stems are filled with papery pith so light that the Indians of the San Joaquin made boats of bundles of them, faggoted together and tied upon a wooden frame.

Year by year the tules reclaim the muddy confluence of the twin rivers. They make an annual growth, die palely, and are beaten down by the wind; between their matted stems the young green comes up again. In the Land of the Little Duck, miles upon miles of them, and not one other thing, stand up on either side the winding water-lanes, man-high and impenetrable.

The Tulare — the place of the tule — is the haunt not only of water-birds but innumerable insect-catchers, and especially of the red-winged blackbirds. In the spring these betake themselves to the reed-fringed marshes in hundreds, building their nests in such neighbourly proximity that the young can hop from rim to rim of the tight-slung, grassy hammocks. Great clouds of the young birds can be seen, just before mating and after nesting in the fall, rising from the low islands of the river-junction. In the season also the male yellow-headed blackbird may be heard singing his sweet but noisy cheering-song to his sombre mate as she weaves marsh grass and wet pond-weed together as a foundation for her home, always prudently completed some weeks in advance of any need of it.

WAITING FOR DUCK—LOS BAÑOS

Where the tules thin out along the moving currents, numerous woven balls of marsh vegetation hang like some strange fruit safely above the summer rise of the waters. These are the nests of the tule wren, built by the industrious male, with who knows what excess of parental care or what intention to deceive. All the while he is at work upon them, in one, the least conspicuous and apparently the least skilfully built, the mother bird nurses the brown nestlings with which, suddenly at the end of July, all the whispering galleries of the tulares are alive.

One who has the courage to penetrate deeper within the tulares, past the crazy wooden landings of nameless ports at which the flat scows put in, past the broken willows where the herons nest and the weedy back-waters lie all smoothly green with the deceptive duck-weed, will see many wished-for sights. Just before dawn and after nightfall the inner marshes are vocal with the varied cries of coot and mallard and the complaining skirl of the mud-hen, the whistling redwing, the bittern booming from his dingy pool, and all the windy beat of wings. But by day a stillness falls through which the clicking whisper of the reeds and the croon of the great rivers cradling to the sea reaches the sense almost with sound. The air is all alive with the metallic glint of dragon-flies; now and then the plop of some shining turtle dropping into the smooth lagoon, or the frightened splash of a marsh-nesting bird, flecks the silence with a flash of sound. Here one might see all the duck kind leading forth their young broods, or the eared grebe swimming with her day-old nestlings on her back. If the day is dark—black clouds with lightnings playing under—one may hear the voice of the loon sliding through his sonorous scale to shaking, witless laughter. Or perhaps the day's sight might be a flock of pelicans on their way to their nesting-ground in Buena Vista, breasting the shallows, and with beating wings driving a school of minnows into some tiny inlet where they may be scooped up in the pouched bills, a dozen to a mouthful. Better still, some morning mist might rise for you suddenly on a strip of sandy shore the cranes had chosen for their wild dances, from which the stately measures of the Greek are said to be derived. Against the yellow sand, as on the background of a vase, the dipping figures and white outstretched wing draperies make the connection clear to you for the moment, along with some other things long overlaid in the racial memory.

Always at evening in the tulares the air is winnowed by the clanging hordes of geese and ducks. Triangular flights of teal wing by you, whizzing like bullets, hazy with speed. Beach-nesting birds, paddlers in the foodful creeks, go seaward. Now and then some winged frigate of the open sea, an albatross perhaps blown inland on a storm, will climb the air to the sea-going wind. Low on the twilight-coloured waters the tule fog creeps in.

You emerge properly from the vast intricacies of the tulares—if you emerge at all, and are not completely mazed and lost in them—at Sacramento, a city but barely rescued from the marsh, and still marsh-coloured with the damp-loving lichens. *La Dame aux Camelias*, to the eye, rich in that exotic blossom as no city in the world, but with a past, oh, unmistakably, and a touch of hectic disorder. The Russians possessed her, and then the breed of Jack Hamlin, and then—but it is unfair to list the lovers of a lady of so much charm and such indubitable capacity for reformation. Sacramento is the State capital, the geographical pivot of the great twin valleys; she divides with Stockton on the San Joaquin the tribute of their waters. It was here on her banks that the overland emigrant trains sat down to wait for the subsidence of waters in the new world of the West, from here they scattered to all its hopeful quarters.

If the part the city has played in history has been that of a hostel, a distributing station, at least she has played it to some purpose. There are few empires richer than the land the twin rivers drain.

VII
THE TWIN VALLEYS

It is geographical courtesy merely, to treat of intramontane California as a valley; it is in reality a vast, rolling plain. Several little kingdoms of Europe could be tucked away in it. North and south it has no natural line of demarcation other than the rivers meeting for their single assault upon the sea, but its diversity deserves the double name. They make, the Sacramento rushing from the wooded north and the sluggish San Joaquin, one of the most interesting waterways of the world. I should say they made, for of the San Joaquin one must be able to speak in the past also, to understand it. One must have seen it before man had tamed it and taught it, supine as a lioness in the sun.

To arrive at a proper feeling for the continuity of the great central plain, it must be approached from the south, by way of the old Tejon Pass, up from San Fernando, or down the Tehachapi grade where the railroad loops and winds through the confluence of the Coast Range with the Sierra Nevada. Here the hills curve graciously about the vast oval of the lower San Joaquin. The downthrow of the mountain, stippled with sage-brush, gives way to tawny sand glistening here and there with white patches of alkali, mottled with dark blocks of irrigated land. Its immensity is obscured by the haze of heat.

One is reduced to the figures of the real estate "booster" for terms of proportion. That modest checkering of green, hours away to the left, is a forty-mile field of alfalfa; beyond it lie the vineyards that in less than a quarter of a century relegated Spain to a second place in the raisin industry of the world. This is the San Joaquin of to-day and to-morrow. The white-tilted vans of the Argonauts saw it as one vast, overlapping field of radiant corollas, blue of lupins, phacelias, nemophilias, gold of a hundred packed species of composite. Wet years it is still possible for the settler in the unirrigated districts to wake some morning to blossomy lakes of sky-blueness in the hollows; from San Emigdio in the Temblors, I have seen, across the whole width of the valley, the smouldering poppy fires along the bluffs of Kern River. On the mesa below Tejon the moon-white gilia that the children call "evening snow" unfurls its musky-scented drifts mile after mile. But the prevailing note of the San Joaquin is tawny russet; gold it will be in the season, resplendent as those idols which the Incas overlaid yearly with fresh-beaten leaf, and in September the barrancas above Bakersfield and Visalia as yellow as brass, but all up and down the hill-rimmed hollow is every lion-coloured tint contending still with the thin belts of planted orchard.

MIRROR LAKE, YOSEMITE

Twenty-five years of cultivation have served to shift the lines of greenness but not greatly to modify the desert key. Once it was all massed in the tulares which fringed the series of lakes and connecting sloughs, continuing northward from the lowest point of the San Joaquin. Kern, Kings, Kaweah, Tule, Merced, and Tuolumne, mighty rivers, and a hundred lesser singing streams fed it. Elk by thousands ramped in its reedy borders. It was a haven of nesting water-birds. Whole islands were populated by pelicans, repairing there annually for the strange, sidling wing-dances that attend their mating. Blue herons nested in the tulares; they could be seen trailing their long dangly legs for hours above the shallows. Indians paddled in their frail balsas, built of papery, dry reeds, down intricate water-lanes in which white men venturing, lost themselves and were mazed to madness. Malaria of a surpassing virulence rode up and down that country on the "tule fogs." Even yet it is the dread of the cities of the plain to find themselves beleaguered by the thick, ghost-white mists that at long intervals roll along the ground, retaking the ancient marshes.

Into this potential opulence the cattleman precipitated himself. He bought—it is more exact to say he acquired—vast acreage of Spanish grants; along the rim of the Coast Ranges, territory equal to principalities was given over to long-horned, lean herds. All about the old beach-line of the San Joaquin may still be seen the remnant of the cattle ranches, low formless houses with purlieus of pomegranate and pampas grass and black figs, and the high, stockaded, acrid-smelling corrals, to mark the receding waves of the cattle industry. On the Sierra side the guttered mesas, the hoof-worn foothills advertise the devastation of the wandering flocks. Early in the 'sixties these appeared, little, long-armed French and Basques, with hungry hordes of sheep at their heels, pasturing on the public lands. They ate into the roots of the lush grass and left the quick rains to cut the soil. The wool in the hand was always worth the next season's feed to the sheep-herder.

AMONG THE REDWOODS OF THE GREAT TWIN VALLEYS

Never was a land so planned for the uses of man, its shielding mountains, its deep alluvial terraces sloping gently to the sun. Men read it in the hieroglyphic the glistening waters spelled between the dark patches of the tulares, but it took some experimenting to read the message aright.

After the cattle and the flocks came the wheat. Up from the meeting waters the land billowed with grain. Owners buckled the ploughs together and drove them with engines by tens and twenties across the thousand-acre fields. But men and engines, they were alike driven by the drouth. In wet years the wheat rancher rode to view his shoulder-high harvest, but when the rains, going high and wide over the valley to break along the saw-teeth of the Sierras, left the wheat unwatered, the same thing happened to the crops that had happened to the cattle and the sheep. And at last, amid the rotting carcases and the shrivelled acres, the message came clear—not the land, but the water. So they shut up the rivers in the cañons and the day of the orchardist began.

Geographically it begins at Bakersfield, below the gap where the Kern comes down from the giant sequoias and is constrained to the wide, willow-planted canals, governed by head-gates and weirs. Such waters as find again their ancient levels, do so by way of the loose sandy soil through which they are filtered in vineyard and orchard. The tulares have been turned under; the elk are strictly preserved in the hope that enough of them will breed to serve the purposes of curiosity. The antelope bands that once flashed their white rumps from bench to bench of the tawny mesas were reduced, the last time I saw them, to a scant half-score roving the Tejon under the watchful eye of the superintendent. But with all this change, nowhere as at this diminished end, does one gather such an impression of the variety, the imperial extent of the San Joaquin. For at Bakersfield is one of the world's largest petroleum fields. The gaunt derricks rear along the unwatered hills like half-formed prehistoric creatures come up out of the ground to see what men are about. Reservoirs, fed with the stinking juices of a time decayed, squat along the barrancas, considering with a slow leech-like intelligence the tank cars in the form of a Gargantuan joint-worm of the same period that produced the derricks, as they clank between the oil-fields and the town. One of the largest oil-fields in the world—and yet the turn of the road drops it out of sight in the valley's immensity!

Bakersfield is a heaven of roses. Doubtless there are other things by which the inhabitants would be glad to have it remembered, but this is the item that the traveller in the season carries away with him. Roses do not die there, they fall apart of their own sweetness, wafts of which envelop the town for miles out on the highway. After nightfall, when each particular attar distils upon the quiescent air, the townspeople walk abroad in the streets and the moon comes up full-orbed across the Temblors at about the level of the clock-tower. Overhead and beyond it the sky retains a deep velvety blueness until long past midnight. Traces of colour can be seen sometimes in the zenith when the glimmer along the knife-edge of the Sierras announces the dawn.

North of Bakersfield, as the valley widens, the Coast Range fades to a mere shadow mountain, the peaks of Kaweah stand out above the banded haze, angel-white like the ranked Host. As the road swings in to the Sierra outposts, broad-headed oaks begin to appear; it skirts the foot of the great Sierra fault close enough for the landscape to borrow something from the dark, impending pines. But for the most part what the observer has to consider is soil and water and the miraculous product of these two. One must learn to think of the land in terms of human achievement.

CLEAR LAKE, LAKE COUNTY

North from the delta of Kern River lies a hundred miles of country scarcely disputed with the flocks, far-called and few, which still at the set time of the year forgather in green swales behind the town for the annual shearing, for the herders to play hand-ball at Noriegas', to grow riotously claret drunk and render an evanescent foreign touch to the brisk modern community. And every foot of that hundred miles is rife with the seeds of life, awaiting the touch of the impregnating water. One holds to that conviction as to a friendly assuring hand. In the presence of that vast plain, palpitating with the heat, the sluggish, untamed water lolling in the midst of it, the white-fanged Sierra combing the cloudless blue, beauty becomes a poor word: appreciation is shipwrecked and cast away. With relief one hails the beginning of a stripe, dark green like a scarf, scalloping the foothills—the citrus belt. From Portersville, Lindsay, Exeter it runs north past the meeting of the waters into the valley of the Sacramento, and for quality and early fruiting sets the figure of the world market. As if its waters had some special virtue, wherever a river is poured out upon the plain some particular crop is favoured. About Fresno it is raisins, at Madera port wine, sherry, and mild muscatel. The Merced, which takes its rise in the valley of Yosemite, is partial to melons and figs. But everywhere are prunes, peaches, apricots, almonds, sugar-beets, alfalfa, unmeasurable acreage of barley, beans, and asparagus. Anything is impressive if the scale be large enough, even a field of onions. Here the league-long rows are as terrible as an army.

Up and down this empire belt proceed two great companies, the hordes of "fruit-hands" and the army of the bees, following its successive waves of fruit and bloom. Gangs of pruners, pickers, and packers are shifted and shunted as the crop demands. Interesting economic experiments transact themselves under the worried producer's eye; alien race contending with alien race. The jarring interests of men have by no means worked out the absolute solution, but the bees have long ago settled their business. They kill the drones and gather the honey for the gods who kindly provide them with hives—the more fortunate perhaps in knowing what their particular gods require.

Wherever along the belt the rivers fail, the pumps take up the work; strenuous little Davids contending against the Goliaths of drouth. They can be heard chugging away like the active pulse of the vineyards, completing the ribbon of greenness that spans from ridge to ridge of the down-plunging hills.

And then one must take account of the cities of the plain! Twenty-five years ago they fringed the Sierra base, mere feeders to the mines, the cattle ranches, the sheep country. They had the manners of the frontier and the decaying, tawdry vices that filtered down from San Francisco, sluiced out by intermittent spasms of reform. They were "wide open." Hairy little herders with jabbering tongues knifed one another in the shearing season, vaqueros "shot up the town" occasionally; it is still within memory that prominent citizen "packed a gun" for prominent citizen. Twenty years ago the last, most southerly, of the chain of settlements was a very cesspool of the iniquities driven to a last stand by the influx of home-seekers. I who went through the years of change with it could tell tales if I would—but, thank Heaven, nobody would believe them! Now in those old places of unsavoury renown rise handsome "business blocks," the true mark of cities.

Homes heaped with roses spread on either side of miles of palm-fringed boulevard. Over it all flows the clear, inspiring current of Sierra-cooled air, sliding down from the ranked peaks that, whitened from flank to flank by perpetual snows, hover like phalanxes of protecting wings.

CASTLE CRAG, RATTLESNAKE CAÑON

Into the very thick of the cities drop down from the high Sierras trails to all its places of delight, the sequoia groves, King's River cañon, and all the lordly peaks about Mt. Whitney and Yosemite; and setting hillward from San Francisco the old Stockton-Sonora road along which surged the undisciplined rout of the gold-seekers of 'forty-nine. It leads, this earliest of valley highways, across the basin of the Stanislaus, past places made famous by the red-shirted, lusty miners, the sleek-coated gamblers of Bret Harte. It passes the twenty-eight Mile House where Jack Hamlin ran a poker game, and many a scene rendered memorable by the gay ladies of Poker Flat. It reaches, by way of a deep-rutted, ancient track, choked with the characteristic red dust of the country, Table Mountain, the home of Truthful James. Table Mountain, having consideration for the near-by Sierras, is a hill merely, with a flat deposit of *malpais*, the "black rock" of regions far north and east. Beyond Sonora lie the old placer "diggings," every foot of which has been combed and sifted for gold. The bones of the earth are laid bare; all the masking clay, tossed and tumbled, clogged with rusty pipes and decaying sluices, lies in heaps and depressions where the gold-seekers cast it. The sense of violation is heightened by the hue of the soil, redder than the hills of Devon, redder than a red heifer—but the river furnishes the more descriptive figure, the martyr hue of the Sacrament. In the flood season it carries the tint of its ensanguined clays far down into the bay's blueness.

The remnant of that riotous life,—the abandoned cabins, the towns falling into dissolution,—like the remaining specimens of the fir and redwood forests cut off to timber the Mother Lode, is left standing by unfitness. The best of it is a little nugget of remembrance of Francis Bret Harte and Mark Twain.

McCLOUD RIVER, UPPER SACRAMENTO VALLEY

It was at Angels in the foothills of Calaveras that Twain, to his everlasting fame, was so impressed with the performance of the Jumping Frog. But life at Angels and all up and down that placer country is as heavy with desuetude as the frog was after the bar-keeper had fed him with buckshot. As well try to get a draught of that old time as a drink at any of the dismantled bars, high, ornate, black walnut affairs across which, in dust and nuggets, passed and repassed probably as much gold as would serve to buy the orange belt of the San Joaquin—and for a figure of magnificence you would find nothing more acceptable to its inhabitants.

Much of the history of that country is written in the names. Here the soft Spanish locutions give place to harsher, but not less descriptive, Americanisms—Jimtown, Jackass Hill, Squaw Creek; the cañons become "gulches," the mesas "flats." Later both of these were overlaid by -villes and -tons, the plain rural names of Anglo-Saxon derivation, Coulterville, Farmington, Turlock. They smell of orchards. Prosperity is coming back on the surface of the fruitful waters, but the redwood forests have not come back. Centuries, nothing less, are required for the building of one of these towers of greenness, and it is barely forty years since all that district was one roaring blast of mining life, rioting, jostling, snatching each from each. In the language of the country, the Italian truck gardeners will "beat them to it." They have smoothed over the old "slickens" and comforted the land with crops.

As one travels north, the bulk of the Sierra lessens, the pines climb higher, the oaks march well down into the middle valley to catch the wet coast winds, the character of the plantations change, there are more grain fields, more neat little farms. Finally the old Overland emigrant trail climbs down from Donner Lake and Emigrant Gap, and you find yourself deep in the Valley of the Sacramento.

By an air-line from the meeting of the waters, its geographical frontier is passed in the neighbourhood of Sonora; perhaps the bridge over the Mokelumne is a better indicator, since that river joins the San Joaquin at the estuary, but it is not until the Overland road is crossed that the character of the country definitely betrays the upper valley.

Ascending the river, the works of man are less and less, the forest and the mountains more. The rapid rise of the wooded slopes keeps the Sacramento troublous. Tributaries, not large but swift and of tremendous volume, pour into it. Occasionally from dark cañons is heard the steady pound of the quartz mill, working some ancient lead, or a smelter blocks out a whole forested slope with its poisonous exhalations; but for the most part the northern valley is given over to brooding quiet, to unending green, and streams as swift as adders.

In Mendocino county, on the coast side, the Range begins to lift toward the snow-line; on the Sierra side the alpine crest shears away. From time to time the "logging" industry cuts a wide track down the redwood forest. One hears above the singing rivers, the clucking of the donkey-engine or the rip of a mill still going in the midst of its self-created, sawdust desert. The glutting of the lumber region has been accomplished as wastefully, as violently, as the search for gold. All up the valley tall prophets of the rain have been butchered to make a lumberman's fat purse. But, link by link, the forestry bureau is closing in the line of the reserves against the lumber "kings," the Ahabs of a grasping time.

The hills fall into a certain order, serried rank on rank. Deciduous growth of the lower slopes gives way to redwoods and Shasta fir. Miles upon miles of them stand so thick that when one dies it does not fall but remains erect in the arms of its brothers. Great columnar boles rise out of the river-basins, soaring high over what, except for their dwarfing proportions, would be a considerable grove of graceful oak and bay and glistening, magnolia-leafed, crimson-shafted madroño. Over these the redwoods rise, as over the heads of worshippers the clustered columns of Milan seek the dome. High up the tops are caught in a froth of pale-green foliage through which the sunlight filters blue. This characteristic refraction from their yellowish, inch-long needles dwells about the redwood as an aura, and far on the horizon distinguishes their ranks from the hill-slopes masked with pines. So, blue ridge on ridge, they advance on the imperious height of Shasta.

DONNER LAKE, ON THE OLD EMIGRANT TRAIL

Shasta is a brother of Fuji and Tacoma, one of those solitary crater peaks whose whiteness is the honourable age of fiery youth, a good mountain dead and gone to heaven. Do not go up on it; you will see a great deal more of what you have seen, wooded hills on hills and perhaps the sapphire belt of the sea, the glitter of lovely, sail-less lakes, but you will not understand it any better, for Shasta has no more to do with the abutting ranges than a great genius with the stock which produced him. This is a prophet among mountains, a vent from the burning heart of creation. One is not surprised to learn that the Indians hereabout count their descent from the Spirit of Shasta and the Grizzly Bear. That dark belt of forest circling the mountain's base looks to be the proper haunt for him, the lumbering, little-eyed embodiment of brute creation. It is well to think of those two things together, the rip of those mighty claws with a ton or two of brute bulk behind them, and the awful witness towering to the blue, and suffer the soul-satisfying fear that lies in wait for man in the great places of the earth. All our modern fears are mean, fears of the common opinion and the bill collector. Shasta will have done its best for you if it enables you to quake in the very marrow of consciousness.

After this it is well to turn southward along the Coast Range, camping by the trout-abounding rivers, losing yourself in the stiff laurels and azaleas of Mendocino, fishing at the clear lakes cupped in the hollows. If the season is right there will be salmon running in Klamath and Trinity rivers or deer in the steep-sided cañons. And everywhere there will be the redwoods. It is not, however, in the crowds that the tree reveals itself. Far down the deforested hills of Sonoma, in isolated groves, in small groups or singles on the tops of bossy, brass-coloured hills, it takes on character and charm.

A redwood grove is a three-story affair. On the ground floor, turned rusty brown, as though the sunlight filtering through had mellowed there a thousand years, creep the wild ginger, the rosy-flowered oxalis, trilliums, and violets. All these lower rooms are crowded with dogwood, with the great berried manzanitas, woodwardias, man-high, and glistening bays, silver-tipped with light. By one of those strange but charming affinities of wild life, the redwood grove is the peculiar haunt of lilies. Every variation of the soil—the peat bogs of the coast, the high sandy ridges, the damp meadows—has each its appropriate variety; and not merely lilies, but droves of them, hundreds of swaying stems, files of them up the line of seeping springs or round the bases of great boulders, lilies breast high, lilies overhead, ruby-spotted, golden-throated, shining white, dowered with the special genius of perfume. Along the chaparral-covered slope and deep within the cañons one tracks them by the subtle, intoxicating scent spreading, as I am persuaded no other perfume does, by a conscious distillation on the melting air.

LAUREL LAKE, UPPER SACRAMENTO

The second redwood story, that wondrous space of blue-diffusing sun, between the deciduous underforest and the fairy web of redwood green, is bird and squirrel haunted. Jays flash back and forth, bright flickers of the humming-bird go buzzing by. Woodpeckers may be heard calling the ever-missing "Jacob, Jacob!" who must in their opinion be concealing himself somewhere about the upper story. The wire-drawn warble of the brown creeper follows the singer up and down the deeply corrugated trunks. Wrens, sparrows, juncos, all manner of little feathered folk in whose coats the tones of brown predominate, frequent the pillared middle rooms. Once I heard what I thought to be a hermit thrush, singing out of the dusk of Muir Wood. But I have not the art of knowing birds by note. People who live much in the redwoods find them silent; I think it might more easily be that the great trunks and green-shot glooms have the same quality of dwarfing sound as size. Redwoods, as I know them, are really lighter and more alive than any other coniferous forests, but the *effect* of umbrageous stillness is induced by vast proportions.

As for what goes on in the upper rooms, who has been there? What birds arise to their three- or four-hundred-foot heights? The few and slight boughs, the feathery layers of foliage rounding in age to sloping crowns, who knows them but the wind and the snows that neither stir nor are stayed by them? There are some matters that the great Twin Valleys keep even from the men for whom they have borne an empire.

VIII
THE HIGH SIERRAS AND THE
SAGE-BRUSH COUNTRY

The proper vehicle for mountain study is not yet available. A great mountain range is like a great public character, there is much more to it than is presented to the observation, and it is not open to familiarity. But if one could fly high and wide over its cloud-lifting summits, one might learn something of its private relations.

From such a vantage it would instantly appear how distinct are the Nevadas (*nieve*, snowy) among the Sierras of California. A very Bonaparte of mountains, new-born and lording it over the ancient ranges, not content with its vast empery but swinging north into the unpre-empted icy regions. San Bernardino and San Jacinto are as far from it as the Faubourg St. Germain from an island in the sea. Sierra Madre is of the Coast Range; Shasta a fire-hole, a revolutionist; the true Sierra is the midriff of a continent. From its northern extremity one sees the sun in a circle and the Northern Lights; that portion of it we know as Sierra Nevada swings into the state above Honey Lake, and ends southward in a tumble of blunt peaks below Kern River. This is quite enough, however, for Californians to make free with, and more than they can appreciate.

Geographically the range begins on the south at Tehachapi, but at Walker's Pass, a day's journey to the north, is the first appearance of its most salient characteristic, the great Sierra Fault. In its youth the range suffered incredible cataclysms. For two hundred miles the great eastern plain dropped; weighted as it was with its withered aristocracy of hills—how weazened and old you can see to this day—it tore sharply downward, and the depth of that fall from the heaven-affronting peak of Whitney to the desert valley of Inyo is a matter of two miles of sheer descent.

The whole Sierra along the line of faultage has the contour of a wave about to break. It swings up in long water-shaped lines from the valley of the San Joaquin, and rears its jagged crest above the abrupt desert shore. Seen from close under, some of these two- and three-thousand-foot precipices have the pitch of toppling waters. As they rose new-riven from the earth their proportions must have been more than terrifying.

Later the Ice Age bore downward from the north, and through immeasurable years carved the fractured granite into shapes of enduring beauty. It rounded the great jutting fronts, it insured them against the tooth of time with the keen icy polish with which they shine still against the morning. It gouged narrow wall-sided cañons, cut the course of rivers, and sinking like a graver's tool into the heart of the range, scooped out deep wells of pleasantness. Afterward, when the ice was old, it must have moved more slowly, for the lines it left, retreating northward, are more flowing, the hill-crowns rounder. And then the mountain was besieged with trees. They stormed it, scaled its free precipices; you can see by the thick mould of the valleys what ranks and ranks of them went down, and along the snow-line how by the persistence of assault they are bent and contorted.

This is the whole effect of the sombre swathes of pine that mask the Sierra slopes. They march along the water-courses, they climb up sheer precipices in staggering files, trooping in the passes; across the smooth meadow spaces they lock arms, they await the word of command. By a very little observation they are seen to be ranged in orderly companies. Here a warm current of air travelling steadily from the superheated valleys carries the life zone higher, there a defiant bony ridge drops it a few thousand feet, but the relative arrangement of species does not greatly vary. The broad oaks, like reverend grandsires, from the foothills see the procession go by, they follow as far as the gates of the mountain, crutched and bowed. All the lower cañons are full of a rabble of deciduous trees, chinquapins, scrub oak, madroño, full of gay camp-followers, lilac, dogwood, azaleas, strumpet penstemons, flaunting lupins, monk's-hood, columbine.

YOSEMITE FALLS

The grey nut pine, wide-branched, unwarlike but serviceable, opens the ranks of conifers. Then the long-leaved pines begin, *ponderoso*, *Coulteri*, and the slender, arrowy, fire-resisting *attenuata*. On the western slope, increasing as they go northward, the redwood holds all the open country, but it is no climber like *monticola*, the largest of all true pines, the captain of the Sierra forests. The firs usurp the water-borders and the low moraines; clannish, incommunicable, they seem not to find it worth while to grow unless they grow stately. Above all these range the thin-barked pines, the lodgepole, Douglas spruce, librocedrus, and hardy junipers in windy passes. About the meadows and lake-borders the quaking asps push like children between the knees along the line; and highest, most persistent, the creeping-limbed, wind-depressed white-barked pine, under whose matted boughs the wild sheep bed.

The trees have each their own voice—a degree of flexibility or length of needles upon which the wind harps to produce its characteristic note. The traveller in the dark of mountain nights knows his way among them as by the street cries of his own city. The creaking of the firs, the sough of the long-leaved pines, the whispering whistle of the lodgepole pine, the delicate frou-frou of the redwoods in a wind, these come out for him in the darkness with the night scent of moth-haunted flowers. But there is one tree that for the footer of the mountain trails is voiceless; it speaks no doubt, but it speaks only to the austere mountain-heads, to the mindful winds and the watching stars. It speaks as men speak to one another and are not heard by the little ants crawling over their boots. This is the "big tree," the sequoia. In something less than a score of forest patches about the rim of the Twin Valleys, the sequoia abides, out of some possible preglacial period, out of some past of which nothing is left to us but the fading memory of the "giants in those days." The age of individual big trees can be computed in terms of human history. There are evidences written in the rings of these that they endured the drouth which made the famine in the days of Ahab the king, against which Elijah prayed. These are growing trees whose seeds are fertile.

One might make a very dramatic collocation of the rise and fall of empires against the life period of a single sequoia, and that would be easier than to transcribe by mere phrases the impression of one of these green towers of silence on the sense. Single and deeply corrugated as a Corinthian column, with only a lightly-branched crown for a capital, they spire for five thousand years or so, and then the leaf-crown becomes rounded to a dome in which the winds breed. Warm days of Spring, their young nestling zephyrs come fluttering down the deep wells of shade to shake the saplings of a hundred years. In Summer the fine-leafed foliage catches the sun like spray, diffusing vaporous blueness; but the majesty of their gigantic trunks is incommunicable. After a while the stifling sense of awe breaks before it, and you go on with your small affairs as children will go on playing even in the royal presence.

BLUE LAKE, LAKE COUNTY

The name *Sequoia* is one of the few cheering notes among our habitual botanical stupidities—an attempt to express quality as it is humanly measured in a name. There was once an American Cadmus, Sequoyah, a Cherokee who invented an Indian alphabet and taught his tribe to read. Seeing them outnumbered in their own territory, he started west with the idea of founding a great Indian empire. He was last seen trailing north across the desert and was heard of no more. Tradition has it that he reached the forest of the upper Kern River and gave the trees his name. At least no botanist with his nose in a book has usurped it.

Forests are for cover. They mask not only the naked rock, but the paths of deer and bear and bighorn. Under the spire-pointed ranks of conifers that look so black from above, verging to blueness, a world of furtive folk goes on. A world of birds is in its branches, squirrels nimble as sparrows, but scarcely anything of this is visible to the watcher on the heights. Rabbits playing on your lawn would be more noticeable in proportion than the seldom-seen bighorn leading his light-footed young from ledge to rocky ledge. The jealous trees cover the trails and obscure the passes.

As you come up through them you observe the flat, soddy spaces of old lake basins, green as jewels, and the hanging meadows gay with cascades of flowers, the stream tangles, the new-made moraines bright with bindweed and sulphur-flower. But from the heights all this lovely detail is hidden by the overlapping tents of boughs. Here and there a stream leaps forth at the falls like a sword from a green scabbard, or higher up, may be traced as the silver wire on which are strung unrippled lakes as blue as cobalt. Great chains of such lakes lead down from the snow-line to the foothill borders, encroached upon by the silent ranks of trees. As they go down they show soddy borders, they tend to fill and to grow meadows where presently deep-rooting trees assume their stations. This is the strategic rule for the taking of a granite mountain. First the grinding ice and the disintegrating water; what the streams wash down collects in the glacier-ploughed basins. It makes lake borders by which the grass comes in—the small grass that is mightier than mountains, that eats them for its food. Lakes at the lower levels become meadows, then trees arrive; they overrun the soddy ground, the snow-manured moraines. The trees themselves take centuries to fruition. At a later stage men dispossess the forest and build cities, but this has not yet come to the Sierras. There is something indomitable in the will of the trees to spread and climb. In the floor of Yosemite and Hetch Hetchy there are hundred-year-old oaks of full form and generous growth, and on the slopes above them the same oaks and of almost the same age are so dwarfed by drouth and altitude that they are not knee-high to a man, but they keep the due proportions of their type. A white bark pine will climb where the weight of the winter drifts is so heavy that it is never able to lift its decumbent trunk from the ground, clinging like ivy to the wall in which it roots.

In the Spring the rich florescence of the conifers sheds pollen in drifts that, carried down the melting water, warn the sheep-herder and the orchardist a hundred miles away of the advancing season. A pine forest in flower is one of the things worth seeing which is most seldom seen, for at its best the high passes are still choked by snow, the lakes ice-locked, the trails dangerous. And then the blossoms, yellow and crimson tassels and rosy spathes, are carried on the leafy crowns high over the heads of the most adventurous foresters. What one finds, as late as the end of June when the trails are open, is a stain of pollen on the lingering snow, and great clouds of it flying wherever a bough is brushed by a light wing. In the autumn the whole wood is full of the click and glint of the winged seeds. Storms of them, like clouds of locusts, are carried past on the wind, to be dropped in the nearest clearing or to find a chance lodging in a moss-lined crevice of the weathered headlands.

LAKE TAHOE, THE HIGH SIERRAS

But from the heights, all feeling for the process of the forest is lost in the sense of its irresistible march—it creeps and winds, it waits darkly for the word. Above the tree-line no sound ascends but a faint vibration, the body of sound making itself felt in the silence. On windless days the forest lies black like weed at the bottom of a lake of air as clear as a vacuum. When the great wind rivers pour about the peaks, it can be seen lashing like weed in the currents, but still almost soundlessly—the roar of it passes down the cañons, and is heard in the cities of the plain. But if the peaks cannot hear what the trees are plotting about, it is not so with the voices of the water. These are sharper, more definitive; they rise re-echoing from the rocky walls and are recognisable each by its distinctive note at incredible heights of the sheer, glassy, granite frontlets.

In the glacial valleys, such as Yosemite, Tehipite, and Hetch Hetchy, where young rivers drop from the headlands in long streaming falls, the noise of them contending with the wind makes mimic thunder. Immense curtains of falling water are tossed this way and that, they are caught up and suspended in mid-air, and let fall crashing to the lower levels. When the wind blows straight up the cañon they will rear against it, and leap out a shining arc, shattering in mid-air like bursting bombs of spray. But later in the season, when the streams are heavy with the melting snows, the wind itself is shattered by the weight of falling water—it exhausts itself in obscuring clouds of silver dust. When from Whitney or Williamson or King's Mountain you can see half-a-hundred such young rivers roaring to the morning, it is as beautiful and as terrifying as the sight of youth to timorous age. They go leaping with their shining shields, and their shouting shakes the rocks. Neither you nor they believe that the most and the best they will come to is an irrigating canal between sober rows of prunes and barley.

Higher than the forests, or the waters rising out of them, is the *Py-weack*, the Land of Shining Rocks. They shine with glacier polish; horses on the high trails sniff suspiciously at their glittering surfaces. Time can lay slight hold on them by thunder, by frost, and the little grey moss; it has not yet subdued the front of Oppapago. Here between snowless ribs and buttresses are the shrunken glaciers that feed the streams, little toy models of the ancient rivers of ice. The snowfields of the Sierras are not so inconsiderable as they seem: they are dwarfed by the precipices among which they hide. Inaccessible to ordinary mountain travel, they make their best showing from the surrounding plains, where, lifted in the middle air, they glow with ethereal whiteness. Close by they display a bewildering waste of broken ice, boulders, and crevasses, made bleaker by the cobalt shadows.

MOUNT SHASTA — SIERRA GLOW

North the line of peaks stretches, broken by the passes that give access to the west. Between them, above the source of streams, in the ice-gouged hollows, lie unfathomable waters that take all their life from the sky. Or perhaps they are reservoirs from which the sky is made, fluid jade and azulite and hyacinth and chrysoprase, as if the skies of many days had run their colours in those bleak bowls. For at this altitude the wave contour of the range comes out most sharply; the sky is strangely deep and darker, as if through its translucence one glimpsed the void of space. One sees the moon and the planets wandering there with pale lamps held aloft.

No life of any sort is visible from here. Farther down toward the coast, over the forested moraines, the condor may be seen leaning against the wind at sunrise. On the edge of the abysmal cañons eagles make their nests and go dropping down the shadowy depths to seek their food from God, but they do not rise to these stark heights. Sometimes a clanging horde of water-fowl, beating up from the Gulf of California overland to the Canadian marshes, will grow bewildered in the face of the great wall-sided cliffs; circling they attempt the forward flight, only to circle and rise anew, until, wing-weary in that thin air, they sink exhausted to the margin of a mountain lake, satisfied at last to thread their way humbly along the creek-beds to open country.

The live forces of the High Sierra are the forces of wind and light. One feels the push of tremendous currents flowing between the peaks as among rocky islands. Day by day they may be charted by the cloud fragments floating on them, by the banners of dry snow dust, streaming out like long grass from the island shores. Thundering fleets of cumuli drift up the wind rivers and assault the great domes of Whitney and Oppapago. The light breaks through all the varying cloud strata, and colours them with splendour; the glow of the clouds reflected on the snow is caught by the watchful mountain-lover far down the valleys of Inyo and San Joaquin. This painted hour of sunset is the apotheosis of mountains, but for me it has less of majesty than the morning after deep snows. These come usually early in the season. The air for days will be full of the formless stir, then the range withdraws itself behind a veil which closes from tented peak to peak, and includes sometimes the parallel desert ranges which lie along its eastern coast. Twenty feet will fall in a single session of the white gods behind the veil. Then comes a morning blue and sharp as a spear-thrust. Every tree is like an arrow feathered in green and white. Airy bridges built upon the bending stems shut in the water-courses; the moraines are smooth and soft as the backs of huddled sheep. By night the range shows from the valley as a procession of winged figures holding the snows upon their bosoms. And that, after all, is the business of mountains. The western front of the Sierra

Nevada, which receives the full force of the Pacific storms, is rewarded with the stateliest forests. Before those extended snowy mountain arms lie the great Twin Valleys; behind them stretches the illimitable sage-brush country, the backyard of the Sierra.

VALLEY OF THE YOSEMITE

"Sage-brush country" is one of those local terms that stand for a type of landscape as distinctive as the moors of England and the campagna of Italy. It means first of all, open country, great space of sky, what the inhabitants of it call "eye-reach," treeless except for a few cotton-woods and willows along the sink of intermittent streams, and stippled with low shrubs of artemesia. This is the true "sage-brush," though it is no sage, the sacred bush of Diana, *Artemisia tridentata*. It may grow in favoured districts man-high, but ordinarily not more than two or three feet in the arid regions which it haunts. Other social shrubs will be found pre-empting miles of the territory to which the artemesia gives its name, *coleogeny*, *pursia*, *dalia*, "creosote," but none other gives it the distinctive feature, the web of pale, silky sage-green against the sun-burned sand.

Other items of the sage-brush landscape are so constant that they are immediately suggested by it: mountains hanging on the horizon in opalescent haze, low flowing lines of hills overlaid by old lava-flows, the "black rock" simulating cloud shadows on the distant ranges, dry red cones of ancient volcanic ash, and great flat table-topped "buttes" of the painted desert.

White-crested ranges on the one hand and buttes on the other mark the limits of the sage; for where snow-caps are, there are trees, and where the buttes begin the cactus and the palo verde reign.

A sage-brush country is a cattle country primarily; perhaps there may be mines; where there is water to be stored for irrigation there will be towns, but the virtue of the sage is that it grows in lands that man, at least, has found no other use for.

It can thrive on an allowance of water that will support no larger thing than a chipmunk or a lizard, and, growing, feeds the cattle on a thousand hills. Therefore it is indispensable to any picture of the sage-brush country that there should be herds at large in it and vaqueros riding, or far down the bleached valley the dust of a rodeo rising. It is impossible to think of such a land and not think of these things, free life, and air as clear and vibrant with vitality as a bell. I can never think of it myself without seeing, in addition, the vultures making a merry-go-round over Panamint, and up from Coso the creaking line of a twenty-mule team.

The sage-brush country of California begins properly at the foot of the Sierras where the state-line sheers east by south from Lake Tahoe. It covers the high valleys that divide the true Sierra from the older, lesser ranges that keep it company as far south as Olancha. Below Mono Lake, that part of the gold region made immortal by Mark Twain, it gives to the chrome- and ochre-tinted soil its distinguishing characteristic. From the long arm of Death Valley it begins to be encroached upon by the mesquite, and at Indian Wells it is driven close under the lee of the last Sierra. The range of which San Bernardino and San Jacinto are outposts carries the artemisia farther desertward, almost to the Colorado River in fact, and south again about the Salton Sea it holds its own with sahuro and palo verde. Its eastern border, like that of the wild tribes along the Mojave line, is lost in pure desertness. Formerly much of that country from San Bernardino to the sea was native to the sage, and all the southern end of the San Joaquin. But now all this is replaced with orchards, for the artemisia proves nothing so much of the soil on which it grows as that, given a due allowance of water, it is as desirable for other things.

THE HALF DOME, YOSEMITE

All this country which I have described to you has so recently been sea that the mark of its old beach-line is plainly to be traced along the east Sierra wall. Still the evaporating water leaves vast deposits of salt and alkali, blinking white in the sink of Death Valley. There are lakes there still where the salt crusts over hard and clear like ice, and deep thick puddles of bitter minerals, the lees of that ancient inland ocean. From the top of any of the denuded desert ranges it is possible to trace the winding bays and estuaries, and, with an eye for location, to choose the points at which one may fairly expect to find potsherds, amulets, fire-blackened hearthstones, and the middens of a nameless people who built their primitive towns along its beaches. It must have had much to recommend it in those days before the sage-brush took it, for this inland sea, rather than the more mountainous Pacific shore, was the route taken by the ancient migratory peoples who left their undecipherable signs scored into the rocks from the Aztec country to the Arctic. On isolated igneous rocks near their old encampments, and high on the walls of the box canons, such as might have been tide-rifts, high above any mechanical contrivance of the present-day Indians, the records resist equally the shifts of sea and sand and the efforts of modern science to read them.

Whether the ghosts of the departed peoples ever revisit the ancient beaches, the ghosts of waters haunt there daily. Morning and mid-afternoon the rivers of mirage arise; they well out of the past and are poured trembling on the plain; phantom fogs blow across them, wraiths of trees grow up and are reflected in false streams. Often in very early light there are strange suggestions of ——dunes and boulders perhaps? Only no boulders in that country are flat-topped like the houses built in lands of the sun, and no dunes are wall-sided. Mirage, we are told, is but a picture of distant things, mirrored on atmospheric planes, but then maybe a ghost is only a mirage deflected on our atmosphere from worlds outside our ken, and it is always easy in the desert to see things that you cannot possibly believe. Whatever they are, mirages are real to the eye. I mean that they are not to be winked away nor dissipated by contact. I have watched a vaquero ride into one of them and drown to all appearances, or seem to be swimming his horse across its billows, all of him below its surface as completely hidden as by rivers of water. Moreover, mirages tend always to occur under given conditions and in the same places. I recall one of the stations on the old Mojave stage road, which, approached from the north about an hour after sunrise, would instantly duplicate: two houses, two lines of poplars, two high corrals.

SHASTA — SNOW CLOUDS

Occasionally along the edge of the sage-brush country one may see that surpassing wonder, the moon mirage, poured like quicksilver along the narrow valleys, as if the thirsty land had dreamed of water.

It is odd how this suggestion of sea and river clings to a country where there is nothing harder to come by than good water to drink. For any other purpose it is not to be thought of. After one of those terrible wind storms, the only really incommoding desert weather, it is possible to find great spaces all rippled and lined in water-markings like a sea that has suddenly undergone a magic transformation into sand. The contours of the desert ranges are billowy; they rise out of the plain like the grey-backed breakers of open sea. The valleys between are narrow and trough-like; the shores of them are lined with crawling dunes that, under the steady pressure of wind currents, are for ever sliding up their own peaks and down the other side, changing place without ever once losing the long slope to windward and the abrupt landward fall of waves.

Another item which adds to the suggestion of the illimitable spread of sage-brush country, like the sea, is the way the sparse forests of the mountain-tops appear to be islanded by it. For the sage-brush extends on across the Great Basin, it stretches into Montana and south to Arizona and New Mexico, it works about the lower end of the Rocky Mountains and well into the great central plain. The ranges lie thick in it as ocean swells, as I have said, and stepping from crest to crest has come the fox-tail pine, *Pinus flexilis*, all the way from Humboldt Mountain to San Jacinto. A sinewy, thinly-branched species, as straight-backed as an Indian, it has little affinity for its noble congeners of the Sierra forests, but keeps to the dry and open ridges, nourished by clouds and by infrequent shallow snows. With it, but at lower levels to which the *flexilis* will never come, is found frequently the one-leaved piñon pine, the food-crop of the wild tribes. But the piñon is a pushing sort, it establishes itself upon the slightest invitation.

There is a story told in the desert of how this grey, round-headed tree was once a very great *capitan*, who, in order that his death might be as beneficent to his people as his life had been, was changed into the foodful pine. Whether the legend is true or not, certain it is that if you sit down by a piñon, wherever found, and stay long enough, you will see Indians. They might come in the Spring looking for *taboose*, or later for willows and grasses for basketry, for seeds of sunflower and chia, to shoot doves by the water-holes or to hunt chuckwallas. A chuckwalla is a lizard, a kind of dragon in miniature, barred black and white, and as offensive to look at as he is harmless, in fact very good eating and not too plentiful. Mojaves, Shoshones, Paiutes, Pimas, all the tribes of the sage-brush country, have this in common, that they live very close to the earth; roots, seeds, reptiles, thick pads of the cholla cactus, even the grass of the field, serve them. They look, indeed, as though they had been made of the earth on the very spot that produced them, of the black rock, the brown sand, and the dark water that collects in polished basins of the wind-denuded ranges.

Very little rain gets past the heaven-raking crest of the Sierra Nevada into the sage-brush country; the most that falls is blown up from the Gulf of California along the draw created by the close, parallel desert ranges. It is precipitated usually under atmospheric conditions that produce violent drops and changes. All that the traveller is likely to find of it is in these rock reservoirs under the run-off of some bare granite cliff, or in the rare, persistent "water-holes" hollowed out by beasts or men, marked in the landscape by one lone tree perhaps, or a clump of shrubby willows. Often there will be no mark at all except the frequency along the trail of skeleton cattle or wild sheep, pointing all in one direction, as they died on their way to the far-between drinking-places. There are districts in this back-door country where evaporation from the body is so rapid that death overtakes the chance prospector even with water in sight or in his canteen across his back. For years a notorious outlaw protected himself in the Death Valley region, by filling in all the springs in a circle about the territory to which he had retreated. Beyond that waterless rim even the law could not penetrate.

And yet how the land repays the slightest moisture! Years when the Kuro-Siwa swings closer to our coast and the winds are friendly, I have seen all that country, from Tehachapi, outside the wall, to San Gorgiono, one sheet of blue and gold. Seeds of a hundred tender annuals lie in the loose sands for years between the shrubby sage, their vitality unimpaired by the delayed resurrection of a chance wet spring. Often I have sifted the sand in my fingers looking for a sign of the life-giving principle which bursts so suddenly into beauty, without finding it. Yet after years in which there is no alteration in the aspect of the country, except the insensible change of the sage tints from grey to green and grey again, the miracle takes place, the blossomy wonder is upon the world.

As a matter of fact, the sage-brush country is by no means the desert that it looks to the casual eye. Besides the social shrubs which have each their own blossom and seed time, even the driest years will afford a few blooms of crimson mallow, and in the shelter of every considerable shrub some dwarfed and delicate phacelia or nemophilia. Even out of dunes which bury its hundred old trunks to the new season's twigs, the mesquite will bear its sweet foodful pods. If you know at what hours to look for it, wild life is never absent, but it is not ordinarily to be found by white men blundering about in broad noon.

It is only when you meet, in the midst of great open valleys wherein there is nothing growing higher than the knees of your horse, and nothing moving bigger than the little horned toad under the cactus bush, bands of Indians well fed, cushiony with fat of mesquite meal and chia, that you understand how little you know of the land in which you move.

There is a Paiute proverb to the effect that no man should attempt the country east of the Sierras until he has learned to sleep in the shade of his arrows. This is a picturesque way of saying that he must be able to reduce his wants to the limit of necessity. Those who have been able to do so, and have trusted the land to repay them, have discovered that the measure is over-full.

A man may not find wealth there, nor too much of food even, but he often finds himself, which is much more important.

INDEX